Winner takes all

The pace finally slows as the third quarter winds down, and the fourth is more of the same. Both teams make runs late in the game, but Herbie makes two great saves for us and their defense doesn't let us in there again. So it ends 1–1.

I sit with Rico on the bus on the way back to Sturbridge. "We should have beat those guys," I say.

"If Pelé up there had half a brain," he says, meaning Joey, who's sitting about six seats up.

"He does," I say. "Maybe even five-eighths."

I shake my head. It's frustrating. Joey's fast, opportunistic. He scores goals and gets girls. But I don't want to be like him.

Well, okay, sometimes I do.

Other Knopf Paperbacks you will enjoy:

RICH WALLACE

SHOTS ON GOAL

A KNOPF PAPERBACK
ALFRED A. KNOPF
NEW YORK

FOUR BROTHERS: BOBBY, JIMMY, BILLY, JEFF
TWO OTHERS: JONATHAN AND JEREMY
FOR YOU

T14595

A KNOPF PAPERBACK PUBLISHED BY ALFRED A. KNOPF, INC.

Text copyright © 1997 by Rich Wallace
Cover art copyright © 1998 by TSM/Jim Erickson

www.randomhouse.com/kids/

Library of Congress Cataloging-in-Publication Data
Wallace, Rich.
Shots on goal / by Rich Wallace.
p.   cm.
Summary: While pursuing his goal of helping his soccer team win the league championship,
fifteen-year-old Bones tries to deal with his resentment of his best friend, on whose
girlfriend he has a crush.
[1. Soccer — Fiction. 2. Friendship — Fiction.] I. Title.
PZ7.W15877Sh   1997
[Fic] — DC21   97-11310

ISBN 0-679-88670-2 (trade)
ISBN 0-679-98670-7 (lib. bdg.)
ISBN 0-679-88671-0 (pbk.)

First Knopf Paperback edition: October 1998
Printed in the United States of America
10 9 8 7 6 5 4 3 2

CONTENTS

1 Stutter-Steps 1

2 Narrating My Life 8

3 A Punch in the Stomach 12

4 Deeswashing 17

5 The First of One Hundred 26

6 Soccer Weather 30

7 Footstepper 34

8 Opportunity 36

9 Nerves 42

10 The Mental Court 56

11 Haircut 62

12 Home 65

13 Eleven Musketeers 73

14 The Methodist Pope 79

15 Sorting Pennies 83

16 Dirt and Sweat 90

17 Little Juke 94

18 The Octoberfest 99

19 Work 110

20 Moving Forward 117

21 Payback 120

22 The Truth 124

23 Halloween 130

24 The Champions 136

25 Twenty Seconds 139

26 Bigger Steps 148

I

STUTTER-STEPS

You sweep it away with the outside of your foot, dodging quickly left, then right, and spurting past the defender. You're as tough as anybody out there, you keep telling yourself, racing now to keep up with the ball.

You need to arc toward the goal, but they're closing in from every angle. You pivot and stumble and the ball bounds away. Now it's whizzing past, waist-high in the opposite direction, and you turn and curse and scramble down the field.

It's mid-September, and the sweat evaporates quickly in the less-humid air. It's easy to breathe hard. You're fifteen, and she's watching, and the blood is close to the surface as you dodge and twist and chase the ball over thick, evenly mowed grass that shines in the slanted light.

Here it comes, shoulder-high but dropping, and you stop it with your chest, bumping it forward and catching it after the first bounce with your foot. Then you've crossed midfield, with running room ahead, and you and the ball and your teammates and the breeze are funneling toward the goal, angling away from the sideline with your chin upraised and eyes open wide.

A stutter-step and an acceleration get you past a defender, and in two more strides you send a long, floating pass toward Joey by the goal. There's contact, a flurry of wrists and knees, and the ball suddenly bullets into the net, beyond the outstretched arms of the goalkeeper.

You drive your fists in exhilaration. Your whole body is a fist, flexed but not tense, and you're as tough as anybody out there. You run and leap and drive your fists again.

You're fifteen and she's watching and you're winning. You're aware of the grass shining in the late afternoon sunlight, of the strength and fatigue in your muscles, and the dryness in your throat you deserve to quench.

Aware of your teammates, of the shouts of the sparsely gathered crowd, and the something in the air that says autumn.

Joey asks me about her after the game, grabbing me lightly above the elbow. "She here to watch you?"

"I don't know." I shrug, pausing, halfway to the locker room. Shannon's standing back by the bleachers with two other girls. She glances my way. My mouth is hanging open.

"You going to the game tonight?" Joey asks, meaning the football game, on the big field downtown.

"Yeah. Why not?" I look around again. She's getting into a car. Joey's started walking again, so I bite on my lip and jog a couple steps to catch him. "You come by for me?"

"I might." Joey's shorter than I am, just as fast, and really is as tough as anybody. He nods. "I'll swing by about seven."

She'll be at the game. Everybody will. I stare at her in the afternoons from the back of the study hall, while she twirls her tawny hair around a finger and reads novels with shiny paper covers. I've seen her watching me, too, as I head for the practice field after school or sit on the hood of a car in the lot.

And I've said hello once or twice, even went as far as "How's it going?" the other day.

She looks at me, too. And she came to the game.

⊗ ⊗ ⊗

I sit on the bench in front of my locker, pulling off my spikes and examining a long new scratch on my knee. There's a cloud of steam rising from the showers and I strip off my jersey, running my fingers through my damp tangled hair.

Guys are snapping towels and laughing, proud; nobody figured on three straight wins. I grab my towel and a tube of shampoo, pushing the green cage locker shut. Joey's got the tape player on and the floor's wet and I can taste dried sweat on my lips.

The water beats down on my chest and the few wiry hairs there look darker, pressed against my skin. The heat loosens my muscles; there's a whole weekend ahead.

I step into work boots and dungarees and a denim shirt. Joey pokes me in the shoulder and says, "That was a really nice pass, Bones. Catch you later."

I've been coming to Friday night football games at this stadium since I was about seven, sitting high in the bleachers with my father. Tonight I can feel the electricity like never before as me and Joey approach from a side street a few blocks away. The school band is assembled; we hear the thin, brassy music in the distance.

"You watch Bugs Bunny tonight?" Joey asks.

"No. My mother doesn't let us have the TV on when we eat."

He stops walking. "How come in almost every one there's this scene where Elmer Fudd or somebody is chasing Bugs, and Bugs runs into a bedroom to hide, and when Elmer busts in, Bugs is standing there in lacy women's underwear?

And then Bugs screams and Elmer slams the door and blushes."

"Sounds familiar." I kind of pull him on the shoulder and we start walking again.

"They had one of the really old ones on," he says. "Porky Pig, of all people, is out hunting and he thinks Bugs gets shot. So Porky tries to do CPR, but he has to pry Bugs's hands off his chest, and when he does, you see that Bugs has a bra on. So Bugs screams and jumps up, and he flutters away like a ballerina or something." Joey puts his hands up and wriggles his fingers and takes some little prancy sidesteps.

"You do that good," I say.

He frowns. "I was demonstrating."

"So, what are you saying? He's . . . what?"

"I think he likes it. I think maybe he bats left-handed now and then."

I shrug. "He's an actor."

"Yeah, but you can tell he's enjoying it. I think he's a transvestite."

I put my hands over my ears and fake like I'm horror-stricken.

We've reached the field. It's bright and noisy, as if all the town's energy is compressed into this bowl. The stands are just about full.

We sit near midfield, ten rows up. I'm wearing a blue windbreaker with the school's name and a soccer ball decaled on the back. The teams are warming up on the field.

It looks like Joey shaved. He's got his glasses on tonight, so he looks kind of refined. He's wearing the same jacket I am.

Shannon's down there by the fence, alone, looking up at the crowd. I catch her eye and lift a finger in recognition, and there's no question that her face brightens. *Any room?* she mouths, and I nod with my whole face and wave her up.

Joey shifts to the left, I shift to the right, and she's sitting where I want her, soft and firm on the concrete bleachers. She's the best contribution to the mix of cigar smoke and powder and cologne under lights that are brighter than daylight.

I try not to smile too wide as she squeezes in, but I'm almost laughing with happiness. She says something to Joey about a history assignment, and he smirks and waves it off. "I'll do it the night before it's due," he says.

She's got on this tan kind of coat and a dark shirt underneath, and she seems somehow livelier than I've ever seen in school. She waves to two of her friends who are walking down below, and they make faces at her like *We can see what you're up to, honey.*

"You played really well today," she says, poking me on the arm.

"Not bad," I say, pumping up a little more.

Fourth quarter comes and we've been laughing for most of the game, me and her. But the Pepsi I bought at halftime needs to escape, so I get up and head for the bathroom, pushing through the crowd.

I bump into Herbie the goalie with some others from the team. "Hanging out later?" he asks.

"Yeah, I'd say so." I've got on a wry kind of smile, hands in the pockets of my windbreaker.

"We're hitting McDonald's after the game. You up for it?"

"Think I'll pass. I got other plans."

"Yeah, I saw you up there with her. Decent."

"Well, I gotta go," I say. "I'll talk to you tomorrow."

I get back to the stands and offer her some M&Ms. She takes two red ones. Our school is ahead by a couple of touchdowns. When the game ends I kind of nudge her. "You wanna, you know, go get something to eat or something?"

She looks a little embarrassed all of a sudden. "Oh. Didn't Joey tell you?"

"Tell me what?"

"Well, I asked him to take me out after the game." She smiles, tilting her head just a bit in consolation. "Sorry."

I look at Joey and my mouth hangs open again. Joey looks down at his shoes, then out at the field.

"Oh," Shannon says in a hurry, "why don't you come along?"

I bite down on my lip, scanning the crowd. "Nah . . . I see Herbie over there. I'll catch up to him and see what's going on. Thanks anyway. See ya."

Sure I will.

I walk down the bleachers and head to where Herbie and the other guys are, glancing back once to see her and Joey walking up toward street level. I stand around while Herbie and the others bust chops, staring out across the field to the highway, at the traffic headed for home.

I inch away from the group, toward the exit at the far end of the stadium. The band is still playing the fight song, but it's far away now. I'm numb.

I shuffle through the excited crowd, out the gate in a hurry. After two blocks I'm clear of the lights and the sounds of the stadium, my boots kicking up the first fallen leaves of the season. I begin to run easy, to get the feeling back, and bite down on my lip.

Joey hadn't said ten words the whole game. I'd been at my best; I had things to say, for once. Her warm brown eyes held some genuine interest. She'd been at the game this afternoon.

I move into the street to pass a guy walking home from the stadium with his little boy, no more than seven.

I pass by the school, dark and closed, and now I'm running faster, hopping the curb to cross a side street. The sweat is starting under my clothes, and I shake my hair back out of my eyes. I dodge quickly left, then right, chin upraised and defiant. A stutter-step and an acceleration get me past the defender, urging the ball ahead, my eyes taking in the whole field but focused on that area of ground between me and the sideline.

There's running room ahead, but they're closing in from every angle. You're tough, as tough as anybody out there, taking in the grunts of the opponents, struggling with unskilled feet to work the ball down the field; so keenly aware of the immediate space you need to conquer, less sharply aware of the goal.

2
NARRATING MY LIFE

My bedroom is in the back corner of the upstairs, across the hall from my brother Tommy's. I'm lying on my bed, staring at the ceiling, thinking about our next game. It's hard to believe that we're 3–0. We went 2–11–1 a year ago. Suddenly we're 3–0.

Nobody can believe it. Not to say that many people have noticed, of course. Not in this town.

We've got our fourth one on Tuesday, a home game against the defending league champions. Last year they shut us out both times, 7–0 and 5–0, when we had five freshmen starting and they had mostly seniors. Now we're sophomores and we're undefeated. But we'll be lucky if forty people show up to watch the game. I've seen forty people at one time in the bathroom at a wrestling match. Sturbridge is a football and wrestling town.

My brother wrestles. Tommy's been varsity since his freshman year; placed second in the state last winter, and he's still only a junior. But he and I are different. Lots different.

Tommy lives in the here and now. He's direct. He makes sense when he talks. I narrate my life as it occurs. I have conversations in my head, and I forget sometimes what I've said aloud and what I've only practiced saying in my mind. I get myself in trouble that way, with girls, with teachers, with my friends.

❁ ❁ ❁

My mother sticks her head in the doorway and smiles at me. "Whatcha thinking about, Barry?" she asks.

"Nothing," I say. "Soccer."

She walks into the room and looks at the pictures on the wall by the window. I've got photographs from every team I've ever been on—two years of Little League, three seasons of Biddy Basketball, about ten seasons of indoor and outdoor soccer at the Y.

"Ever talk much with Carrie?" Mom asks, pointing to a girl kneeling next to me in one of the soccer photos.

I shake my head. "No."

"Seems like a nice girl." This is a nudge, but I won't bite.

"I guess," I say. "She's going out with a senior."

"Oh." She turns toward me and smiles again, brushing back her hair, which is dark and sort of curly. She's worried about me. I'm too into sports, I only have one close friend, I spend a lot of time in my room with the door shut, and I've never had a girlfriend. That's what she sees, anyway.

"Come downstairs soon," she says. "Don't waste a Sunday afternoon."

She leaves and I get up and close the door. I sit on the bed and look at the wall.

Joey's in just about every picture; his father coached everything and I almost always landed on his team because me and Joey have been best friends since second grade. But it was never Joey's team, or my team, or the Sharks or the Jets or the Blasters—whatever the official name was that season—it was Bones-and-Joey's team. Always. An inseparable partnership.

Joey was the star of those teams, scoring lots of goals, making the lay-up off the fast break, driving in the winning run. I was the guy who made Joey look good, taking the outlet pass and finding him in the clear, or crossing the ball in front of the goal so he could knock it in.

I'm still doing it. He's got five goals this season and I've assisted on four of them. It also looks like he's got a girlfriend, and I think I deserve a double assist for that one. The jerk.

My life has been lived within two shadows: my brother's and Joey's. Even my name, what everybody calls me and doesn't really fit, came from Tommy. His first sentence, the legend goes, was "Boney wet," Boney being his fifteen-month-old pronunciation of Barry. It stuck, although I've never been particularly boney. I'm five-foot-seven, 140.

Joey's shadow is different. He and I have always been there for each other. Until the other night, I mean. First fight I ever got in was during second-grade recess. We were playing touch football and I was mostly blocking. This kid Steven Bittner—who was twice my size—kept trying to punch me in the nuts to get past me. Finally I got mad enough and swung at him, and he whacked me good in the teeth. Then he pinned me down and had his knees on my shoulders, and Joey yelled, "Let him up, you pig!"

Steven turned his head to look at Joey, and I started squirming like crazy to get out from underneath.

"Let him up," Joey said. "He can't fight like that."

So Steven started to get off me. He was big and slow, and I was small and fast. I got to my knees real quick and caught him square in the nose with my fist. By then some teachers had noticed the commotion and started running over. Steven and I had to stay in for the next week of recesses, but he never bothered me again.

Joey's always been a half-step ahead of me in sports, but we've been on even ground in everything else.

He just took a step past me with Shannon, though. And I don't think that's fair.

3

A PUNCH IN THE STOMACH

The rain starts while we're warming up, standing in a semi-circle and firing shots at Herbie. I sneak a look down the other end of the field, where the Greenfield guys are working a wheel, running clockwise around the man in the center, sending the balls back and forth from the center to the rim. They're good.

There's no joking today, no comments about Herbie's cigarette breath or Rico's big nose or Dusty's lisp. This game means too much, more than anything. Two undefeated teams: 3 and 0.

"Kick some ass!" yells Joey, sending a ball into the high corner of the net.

"Everything you got!" hollers Trunk, booting a line drive that Herbie leaps for and bats down.

"We're Number One!" shouts Herbie, picking up the ball and squeezing it. "We're it, man!"

Herbie tosses me the ball and I catch it on my thigh, bouncing it up and juggling it on my other foot. I give myself a lead, plant my foot and fire, and listen to the thud as the ball hits the crossbar and bounces back.

The Greenfield guys are broken into pairs now, shadowing each other up and down the field, one guy dribbling, the other one backpedaling. They've got more players back from last year than I thought they would. A lot of good players.

The coach calls us over; we gang up around him. My hair

is wet but my throat is dry. The officials are huddled up at midfield. The Greenfield players run over to their sideline, leaping and yelling.

I close my eyes for a second. It's still early season, there's a long way to go. But those Greenfield guys are ready to clobber us, to beat us as bad as last year. It shouldn't really matter so much. Shouldn't make me so nervous.

We've got three wins already, but that holds no water against these guys. This game is the measuring stick. Our program is four years old, and we've never even scored against Greenfield. That's eight straight shutouts.

I look around at Rico, at Herbie, at the others. The coach clears his throat. "Last year," he says slowly, "was a long, long time ago. . . ."

Minutes go by before I finally touch the ball, intercepting a centering pass in front of our goal. I step left, then go right, creating space and moving down the field. I feed Joey on the run and he moves past the center line, dribbling into a mass of green-and-white shirts. "You can't do it alone," I holler, but he tries to anyway, and quickly loses control. I hustle back as the ball flies into our end.

Up and down the field, neither team penetrating for most of the first quarter, until their striker finally breaks ahead of the pack and crosses the ball to a midfielder, who one-touches it right back and the striker boots it into the upper corner of the goal.

I let out my breath in a huff and a cloud of moisture swirls up and away. Herbie punches the ball to the official, and Joey yells, "Let's get it back!"

Coach claps his hands and I wipe my forehead and jog back into position. "Let's go!" I yell, as much to myself as anyone else.

At the half we're still down 1–0, but we've had some opportunities, this one's within reach. Coach tells us midfielders to bear down and gut it out—get back on defense and keep sparking the offense. My arms are fatigued, even more than my legs for some reason; maybe it's from tension, from the weight on our shoulders.

But the Greenfield players are tired, too. The momentum shifts our way in the third quarter. A couple of shots on goal, a couple of close misses. Finally we've got a corner kick. Dusty floats it just in front of the near post and their goalie leaps to grab it. But the wet ball slips through his fingers and it's all he can do to bat it free as he goes down. It wobbles to the left of the goal and I'm there, an open net in front of me, and a surge goes through me as I connect, and it soars, and it powers into the net like a punch in the stomach of our opponent.

They mob me. It's tied. Joey hits my shoulder hard enough to bruise it, and big Trunk lifts me off the ground in a bear hug. I break free and "Yes!" and race back to our end of the field. People on the sidelines are yelling. Herbie's on his knees in front of our goal, facing skyward with his eyes closed. It's tied.

We're on a new level now. We weren't really sure about ourselves, not ready to admit that we're as good as anybody in this league. But now we know it, now we can prove it if we can just get that ball through this defense again. Back and forth through the fourth quarter, neither team gaining much, neither team yielding. My nose is running and I suck it up and spit it out in a rapid wad. Eyes on the ball, eyes on the ball. Drive, drive, drive . . .

We can beat these guys, but it has to happen now. I'm soaked but warm, my legs splattered with mud and my hair matted to my head. The rain is steady but light, so the footing hasn't been bad until the past couple of minutes.

Joey's taking a throw-in near midfield; guys are shouting and pushing to get clear; there's three minutes left in a 1–1 game. Teeth are clenched and elbows locked.

"Bones!" he yells, but his throw bounces four feet in front of me and strikes me in the knee. *Throw to the feet, Joey!* The guy marking me takes the ball and I slip again, catching myself with my hands. I push back up, but the ball's already gone.

This is the guy who scored their goal, heading back upfield now. He chips it toward the middle, lobbing it over a defender, and they've got a guy in the clear zeroing in on Herbie. Herbie dives toward the corner, but the ball beats him there. Like that.

The Greenfield players go wild. I mouth an obscenity and wipe my hands on my soaking blue jersey. "Throw to the feet," I say to Joey, but it's too late. And I should have controlled it anyway.

Time races away now. We can't mount a decent attack. We blew it. We had at least a tie, but we blew it. Herbie blocks a shot and boots it high and long, but the ref blows the whistle before it hits the ground.

We ain't undefeated any longer.

⊗   ⊗   ⊗

My brother's standing on the sideline when we walk off, hands in the pockets of a yellow windbreaker with the hood up. He's fifteen months older than I am, fifteen pounds lighter, two inches shorter, and three times as strong. I don't run in the same circles he does.

"Nice," he says, taking out one hand to shake mine. "Tough one."

"Sucked," I say, but I know we didn't. It makes me feel better that Tommy knows it, too. Coach is calling us over, huddling us up.

Turning point, the coach is saying. The first real test and we held up like champions. We're not doormats any longer. We'll see these guys again.

There's steam rising from my hands. Everybody looks like they've crawled through a swamp. I wipe my nose with my sleeve and chew on the side of my lip.

Coach reminds us that Greenfield's a perennial power. We've got seven sophomores starting, three juniors, and a senior. There's a lot of glory ahead.

Everybody's quiet. We wanted this game bad. We almost had it, too. When is the rematch?

4

DEESWASHING

I get dressed in a hurry and yell to Joey to move his butt. We'll get dinner at work. It's slow on Tuesday nights; I might even get my homework done if Carlos isn't around. Kenny doesn't care.

Work is the kitchen of the Sturbridge Inn: scrubbing pots, running the dishwasher, making the coffee. Six till we get done (they stop serving at ten) Sunday and Tuesday. Sometimes on Saturday if there's a reception or something.

My brother worked here all summer and he got me and Joey these jobs last month when some guys left for college. Tommy waits on tables for weddings and banquets.

Carlos is in his office when we punch in, but he's getting ready to leave. "Hello, boys," he says. "It will be slow tonight, so you will have time to straighten up the walk-in and the storage closet."

We head for the back of the kitchen and Joey tries to imitate Carlos's accent. "You run the deeswasher, I'll scrub the pots."

"Real funny," I say.

We check the walk-in refrigerator. Kenny's in there drinking a can of beer. He hides them behind the crates of celery and stuff, but he usually waits until Carlos goes home before he pops one open.

"Hey," he says real slow when we walk in. Kenny's about thirty-eight, and he's been working in this kitchen for twenty years. He had the same job we have until a year ago, when they decided he'd learned enough to cook on slow nights. It's an easy menu; I could handle just about everything on it—steaks and pork chops and fried shrimp. The toughest item is veal cordon bleu, and that's no big deal once you've seen it a few times.

"Starting early, huh?" Joey says to Kenny, meaning the beer.

"Just the one," Kenny says. "He still out there?"

"Was when we came in," I say. I start picking through a crate of lettuce on the floor, looking for rotten ones. Two of them are getting slimy, so I peel off the bad leaves and toss the heads back in the box. Kenny watches me. He's got slick brown hair combed over to cover a high forehead, and dark-rimmed glasses. He's short, thin except for his gut, and always wears a plain white T-shirt. "You boys win today?" he asks.

"Just about," Joey says. He's taking tomato wrappings out of a box on the shelf. The tomatoes come individually wrapped in blue tissue paper, and most people leave the paper behind when they need tomatoes. So sometimes you have to dig through six dozen tomato wrappings minus one to find the last tomato in the box.

It's one of our duties on Tuesday nights to keep the salad bar full, so we know what it's like to have to find the last tomatoes.

"We're gonna eat as soon as Carlos leaves," Joey says to Kenny. Then he steps out into the kitchen and I follow. You don't want to be alone in the walk-in with Kenny.

We start with a load of lunch dishes that the day shift walked out on. You put them on trays and they run along a conveyer belt through the dishwasher. But you have to scrape all the crusts and uneaten cole slaw and other glop into the garbage first or it will gum things up. And the silverware has to soak in this blue stuff or it won't come clean. You wind up doing some of the silverware by hand anyway if it's got pancake syrup or dried ketchup on it.

After a while I make a club sandwich the way Carlos taught me: take three slices of bacon from the pile (if you get breakfast here you could be eating reheated bacon that was cooked twenty-four hours before) and put it under the broiler for a few seconds. Make three slices of medium-brown toast, spreading the bottom one with a thin layer of mayonnaise. Put the bacon, three slices of tomato, and two lettuce leaves on the bottom piece of toast, add the second piece of toast, then spread some mayonnaise on that one. Put on about a half-inch layer of thin-sliced (THIN!) turkey breast, and cover with the third piece of toast. Put four of those toothpicks with the swirly plastic things on the ends through the whole thing (to hold the pieces together when you slice it), then take a big knife and trim off any lettuce that's overhanging the bread. Gently support the sandwich with the fingers of your left hand, and carefully cut it into four triangles by slicing from corner to corner.

I offer to make one for Joey. He says no. He takes two pieces of bread, spreads one with mustard, throws on a clump of turkey, puts on the other slice, and mashes it all down with the heel of his hand. Then we go to the storage room to eat.

We sit on cardboard boxes on the floor and talk about soccer. We've got another game in two days.

Joey's got short dark hair and is solid all over, but he's not very big. My mother says he's handsome. She says he's like her third son, since he's spent so much time at our house, playing one-on-one basketball in the driveway or playing video games or just hanging out in my room. She's always asking me if he's got a girlfriend, but what she really wants to know is whether I have a girlfriend yet. If I did I wouldn't tell her.

Joey claims he had no idea Shannon was going to ask him out at the football game. I told him he sucks anyway, because he didn't have to accept. He knows damn well I was after her. And I would have helped him out if the situation was reversed.

At least I think I would have. Maybe not.

Joey's parents pressure him to excel; his mother insists on honor-roll report cards, and his father absolutely lives to see Joey's name in the sports section. He used to do things like have their last name printed on the back of Joey's Little League jersey, or call the newspaper when his son scored a goal in a YMCA game. Like anybody cared what a nine-year-old did.

The result is that Joey can't ever relax when the subject is sports. As talented as he is, I feel sorry for him because he can't totally appreciate it when he does something good—his father robbed that from him. So I turn the conversation to music or girls or television whenever I can. Joey needs a break from the intensity.

"We've gotta work on our ball control in the box," he says. "We get the ball in there, but there's no coordination. It's like every man for himself."

Strange that he would say that, since he's the worst offender. But at least he's aware of how out of sync we can be.

"I mean, I can pull it off, but some of our guys don't have a clue."

That sounds more like Joey: arrogant and selfish. Even though it's true.

I'd say there are at least five guys on the team with more natural ability than Joey has. They're faster or stronger or more agile, or all of those things. But Joey would kick anybody's butt one-on-one. I wouldn't tell him so, but I have to admire that.

Kenny comes into the storage room and looks around. He reaches for a can of olives and turns it over in his hand. Then he sets it back on the shelf. "Got dishes piling up out there," he says.

Joey rolls his eyes at me. "We'll get to 'em," he says.

Kenny just sort of grunts. "We ain't paying you to sit on your ass," he says, turning to leave.

Joey scrunches up his face and sneers. He raises one eyebrow at me and gives a laugh. "Big shot," he says quietly.

"Hey, he's earned it," I say.

"Yeah, I guess I'm just jealous," Joey says. "I want his job, you know. That's my career objective."

"You and me both," I say.

"Gotta admit, you work your butt off every day washing dishes for twenty years, you deserve a lot of respect."

"No question about it," I say.

"I only hope I have the tenacity to stay with it that long," he says. "Someday, boy, someday. I'll be the guy who gets to fry hamburgers, the man who can maintain this place's fine reputation for baked potatoes."

"And I'll be there with you," I say. "You and me."

"We'll be heroes."

"Like Kenny is to us."

"God bless him."

Seth the blond busboy brings in the last load of dishes at about quarter to ten, so we run them through the dishwasher and go in the back to start on the pots. There aren't many, but we're bored and want to get out of there. I dump some liquid soap into the sink and run the hot water on full, and Joey starts scraping out a giant roasting pan with a spatula. Carlos made meatballs in there this afternoon, and there's a crust of baked-on grease and tomato paste.

"Why the hell didn't they at least let this soak?" Joey says, though he doesn't say who "they" are.

"They is us," I say. "It was sitting there when we came in."

"Well, we suck then," he says. "This shit is welded on there."

"Dump some water in it until we finish these others," I say. "It'll soften up."

But after we've scrubbed the other pots the giant one is not coming clean. We've gone through three heavy-duty Brillo pads on it, but there's still a mound of tar in the corners.

"You dump the garbage yet?" Joey asks.

"Not the one by the dishwasher."

"Get it."

I carry it over and Joey picks up the roasting pan, and we go out the back door to the Dumpster. Joey sets down the pan. He opens the lid of the Dumpster and we get hit with the sweet smell of rotting garbage. It's sort of nauseating, but sort of pleasant, too. The rats like it, anyway. Joey gently sets the pan between two full plastic trash bags. Then he takes the garbage bag from my hands and lays it on top. He nods to me and breaks out in a big stupid grin.

We mop the floor real quick. Kenny's asleep in Carlos's chair in the office. He opens one eye when I punch my time card and mumbles, "See you, boys." We get out of there in a hurry.

You can't do much after a shift at work because you feel greasy from head to foot. So there's no sense hanging out. But if you go home to shower you don't get allowed back out, so we usually stop at the Turkey Hill store for some soda, then maybe spend ten minutes talking to Herbie and anybody else who's still on Main Street.

But Joey stops on the sidewalk in front of the bakery and says, "You know Shannon?"

I look at him like I can't believe he would ask such a stupid question. I don't say anything.

"You know her friend Eileen?" he asks next.

"Yeah." I know Eileen. She's okay. She's not Shannon.

"I need you to go out with her."

"What?"

"Not go *out* go out, just go to the football game with her. With me and Shannon."

"Why?"

"To keep the conversation up," he says. "You know. I don't have that much to say. You talk to her good."

"To Eileen?"

"To Shannon. You set her up for me."

I shove him on the shoulder, not real hard, and stare at him without knowing what to say. "You suck," I finally tell him. I shake my head and start to walk. "You suck."

"I'm not asking much," he says, following me. "Just come with us to the game. Friday night. You can ditch her afterwards."

I keep walking. "The game's away this week," I say.

"Next week, then."

"See you tomorrow," I say.

"I'll tell Shannon to tell Eileen?" he calls.

"We'll see." I start jogging, to get away from him, to get home. I need a shower. I need sleep.

Sturbridge: An Insider's Guide
By Barry Austin

Down the end of Sixth Street, behind
the abandoned garment factory, is a
four-foot-wide pedestrian bridge
across the Pocono River. The river is
forty feet wide here and a few feet
deep, with deeper pools where you
might catch a trout if you want to
fight your way down the steep, over-
grown banks.

Some evening when you're about
twelve, you and your best friend might
get a couple of his uncle's fat cig-
ars, and you'll sit on the bridge in
the dark and light up. Nobody comes
by here much at night, so if you're
quiet and respectful you probably won't
get hassled.

You can puff away for an hour, chaw-
ing the cigar down to a stub while
watching the river go by.

Later on, make sure you've got the
wind at your back when you lean over
the railing to puke.

5

THE FIRST OF ONE HUNDRED

Herbie and I came up with this idea tonight, and we're pretty excited about it. We figure it will be quite an honor when we finally bestow it.

The Hundredth Asshole (in fact, all one hundred of them) must meet our carefully selected criteria (which change according to the individual). And they must pass directly in front of or behind this bench (driving, walking, running, Rollerblading, skateboarding, or cycling—maybe by other means, but we can't think of any) when both of us are present. So far we've counted seven (which includes Brendan Doherty only once, even though he cruises past in his car every six minutes or so). You can only be counted one time. Brendan Doherty, however deserving he may be, will never be known as the Hundredth Asshole.

Brendan, who's a senior, qualifies for a whole lot of reasons. In particular because he constantly talks about how much sex he gets, but everybody knows it isn't true.

Then there's Mr. Brosnan, the banker, who got counted about an hour ago. When we were little, he coached his son Frank's sports teams and was even worse than Joey's father. He did everything in his power to make Frank the star (and also to make the kid miserable, since we all grew to hate his guts). Now Frank won't go near a sports field. And he's not a bad kid, either.

Mrs. Furman was number seven. She calls the newspaper's

"Sound Off" column every other week to complain about kids hanging out on Main Street. You can tell she's called because she starts every message with "I don't mean to be a complainer, but . . ."

Footstepper walks quickly by on the other side of Main. I look at Herbie and he shrugs and shakes his head. "Don't know," he says.

Footstepper's a junior. I've never heard him speak. Footstepper walks fast, with long skinny strides and his hair in his eyes. Nobody knows much about Footstepper. So the count stays at seven.

The great thing about this idea is that it's so random. You have to fit the criteria to win, but being the hundredth to qualify will be pure chance. We know that a truly deserving Sturbridgiot will capture that moment.

We expect to have a winner within a month.

We start talking about soccer; we tied Laurelton yesterday. Herbie's going on about this goalie from the Mexican national team that he saw on ESPN last weekend. "I'm not kidding," he says, playing with his lighter, watching the fluid twirl around in the little plastic tube. "They're down by a goal and this goalie comes running all the way down the field—all the way to the other goal—and almost heads it in on a corner kick. It was nuts. And it almost worked."

"You should do it," I say.

"I might." He looks straight up into the air, like he's checking the clouds. "Coach would kill me."

"Yeah." I look up, too. "What are you looking at?"

He just shakes his head. "Nothing."

I don't quite get Herbie yet. We've never been in the same class or anything. People were surprised when he came out for soccer last year, because he hadn't been into sports before. He got laughed at the first few times he played goalie in practice, and the seniors used to hide his shoes and put Ben-Gay in his jock. But he's got an instinct or something that makes him zero in on the ball, even if it's fired at him from close range. So he's starting in goal for us and doing pretty well.

I look up Main Street toward the traffic light, then down toward the diner, making sure Joey isn't on his way. "Herbie, you know that girl Eileen?"

"Eileen Hankins?"

"Yeah."

"Some."

"You know anything about her?" I ask.

"Some. Why?"

"No reason. You know Shannon?"

"Joey's chick?"

"Is she?"

He laughs a little. "He thinks so."

"Oh."

Herbie's got bad skin, but everybody likes him. There isn't anybody in the whole tenth grade who doesn't think he's cool, because he can bring out the bad side of anyone. He's gotten a lot of kids in trouble; not big trouble, just like detentions and warnings from the cops. You appreciate that sort of help, because most kids don't want to get in trouble on their own, but they do want the status that goes with it.

"I don't know if *she* thinks she's his chick," Herbie says.

"She asked him out."

"Yeah, but she'll break his chops sooner or later," he says. "She moves around."

I scratch my ear and stare across the street at the travel agency. I'm thinking hard.

"You might get a chance," he says.

"You think?"

"Give it time. I mean, how long could she want to hang around with Joey? You got some animal magnetism; just watch for an opening."

I start to say something else, but Herbie knocks my arm and jabs his finger toward a gray van that's driving past. "Number eight!" he says. "That guy's my father's supervisor at the plant. The bastid."

6
SOCCER WEATHER

If you want to know why I play soccer, days like today are a big part of the reason. We won again yesterday—shut out Weston South three–zip—so we're loose. We're 4–1–1, and it's the type of day you just want to sprint up and down the field and holler.

The sun is warm on your bare arms, but there's a light, cool breeze. It's so bright you have to squint when you face the sun, but everything is clear. You can hear the ball rolling through the grass, a fast swishing sound, and the trees in the hills around the field are turning red and orange and yellow. No clouds, not even wisps.

This is soccer weather. The ball's coming at me and I settle it, turn and go. I should pass, but this is only practice and we're scrimmaging the JV. So I throw some moves at the guy racing toward me and I'm past him in a second. Even dribbling the ball I'm faster than most of these guys, and I give a couple of jukes and get inside the defenders.

It's me and the goalie. He crouches and inches forward; I dodge left and shoot. He dives and gets a hand on the ball, but it barely changes the trajectory. The net ripples as the ball hits it hard. I slap hands with Rico. I trot back to our end.

Yesterday was beautiful. I had an assist in the first quarter and a goal in the second. Joey comes straight down the middle just before halftime and the defenders close in on him. I'm level with Joey to his right, going full speed.

Usually he'll force the shot anyway, but this time he squirted it just past their guy, and I didn't have to trap it, didn't even break stride, just planted with my left foot and fired with my right. The goalie had no time to react.

My father was at the game, standing on the sidelines in a suit, and I caught his eye after I scored. He waved with his fist and said "Way to go," but I don't think he gets it. He wasn't into sports as a kid, so he can't really understand, can he?

We take a break and Trunk's little brother comes running over with the Scranton paper. "Greenfield lost yesterday," he says. Joey grabs the paper and says, "Holy shit. East Pocono beat 'em. So we're like right back in it."

"Forget that," Coach says. He frowns, rubbing his chin, which has reddish whiskers like sandpaper. "We just need to keep winning games. You can't be concerned with what the other teams are doing. We get Pocono next."

"We'll kick their asses," Herbie says.

"Don't talk about it," Coach says. "Do it."

"They got the league standings in there?" Herbie says, trying to take the sports section from Joey.

Coach blows his whistle. "Break's over," he says.

"Check it out!" Herbie says. "We're tied for second."

"I said to forget that," Coach tells him.

"We can win the league," Herbie says, still studying the paper. Everybody else is moving slowly onto the field.

"Break's over, Herbie."

"In a second, man."

Coach blows his whistle again, louder and longer. "Are you stupid, Herbie? Five laps."

"For what?"

"For being a wise ass. Get running."

Herbie shrugs and laughs and starts running, real slow.

"Get moving," Coach says. "No pain, no gain."

Herbie keeps jogging, looking over his shoulder at Coach. "No goal, no disappointment," he says.

In the locker room we get a better look at the standings, and it does look pretty good:

	W	L	T
Greenfield	5	1	0
East Pocono	4	1	1
Sturbridge	4	1	1
Laurelton	2	1	3
Weston North	3	3	0
Midvale	1	4	1
Weston South	1	4	1
Mount Ridge	0	5	1

We want to win the league more than anything, but there's a bonus if we get it. If you win the league, you get an automatic berth in the regionals. There are five leagues with automatic berths for their champions, and everybody else gets thrown into the mix for the three at-large bids. The at-large teams are always from over in the valley by Scranton; that's where the power is. Our league's never done jack in the playoffs. We're planning to change that over the next few years.

So we've got East Pocono next, and the winner keeps

pace with Greenfield. We have two nonleague games next week, then we play everybody in the league once more. We've gone from last place a year ago to contenders this season, and it's only going to get better.

That's another reason I play soccer. I like to win.

7
FOOTSTEPPER

Wednesday night. My brother drives past and beeps the horn, but no way is he going to stop. He's got a carload of his wrestling buddies and they're headed for Weston. As if there's anything to do over there, either.

The count is up to forty-one. Herbie insisted on including two of the guys in my brother's car. I agreed, even though Tony Terranova isn't such a bad kid. He just locked Herbie in a gym locker once when we were freshmen, so Herbie's got an understandable grudge.

Joey hasn't shown up yet, but Herbie's been here since after practice. I don't know if he ever goes home. He's been a fixture on this bench since last summer.

I've got a can of Coke and a package of little chocolate doughnuts from Turkey Hill, but Herbie doesn't want any. Joey might be with Shannon, but I doubt it. I asked him if he was still seeing her. He said I guess so. I never see them together. I see her looking at him.

"Coach reamed me out again after practice," Herbie says.

"How come?"

"He says he heard I was smoking in the bathroom. Would I do that?"

"Never," I say.

"He said he'd kick me off the team if he catches me."

"So don't get caught."

"I don't plan to."

"Why don't you quit?"

"The team?"

"Smoking."

He just shrugs and smiles with half his mouth. "I might," he says. "But it will be my idea when I do."

This end of Main is where anything that might happen would happen. Freshmen congregate down near the diner, and junior high school kids are all the way down near Rite Aid. I'm just getting used to hanging out up here, in front of the boarded-up movie theater.

I'm not sure when the last time something happened was. I'm not sure anything ever happened here. But we'll be ready if it does.

Herbie yells "Footstepper!" as the guy walks by on the other side of Main. Footstepper gives a sheepish grin and a sort of wave—spreading out the fingers of his left hand. But he doesn't slow down.

One time in school I ran into Footstepper in the bathroom. He came out of a stall while I was combing my hair at the sink. I moved aside and he washed his hands, then he took a paper towel and dried them. He was a lot taller than me and had wispy sideburns. Then he left.

We play East Pocono tomorrow, over there. Here comes Joey. Alone. What's the deal with him? He needs to move in or move out. I want her more than he does.

8
OPPORTUNITY

Midfield: You're part of the offense, part of the defense. Always involved. I live for days like this.

We came in fired up, ready to take control of this league, but East Pocono jolted us early. Precision passing, great teamwork, speed. They scored in the first minute.

"Settle down," I say. "Think." But they're back on the attack already, working toward our goal, slicing in from the sideline. A shot, low and hard, and Herbie dives for it, gets a hand on it, deflects it out of bounds.

"Jesus," I say. "Form a wall!"

One of their wings rushes over for the corner kick. He chips it toward the front of the goal. Hernandez gets a thigh on it but fails to control the ball. It's loose, bouncing to the side, and Herbie's on the ground, rolling on the ball, wrapping it up and leaping to his feet.

He punts it, high and long and off to the right, so I run down the field, on offense again. But Joey takes it and races along the sideline, head down. Finally he just overruns the ball; East's got it back. It's passed to my side, and their wing is in front of me, angling toward the goal.

Squeeze him toward the sideline, don't give him a lane. He feints left, takes it right, but I get a foot on it, send it out of bounds.

"Mark up!" I holler. He takes the throw-in, propelling it along the sideline toward the corner. There'll be a centering pass now, back toward the guy who took the throw; I know it's coming before I can think. And I'm there, knocking it downfield and chasing past the wing.

Down the sideline; two guys trap me but I pivot and spot Rico. He dribbles twice, returns the ball to me near midfield, and I've got room ahead, I'm on the run.

Everyone's racing this way now, but I've got the jump on them. I center it back to Trunk, he advances it to Dusty, and I'm curving in from the sideline, their defenders are coming up.

Trunk's got it again at the top of the penalty area and he slips it toward me in the clear. My eyes open wide, it's just me and the goalie. But the whistle blows before I get to the ball. I'm offside.

"Damn." But it's okay. We've changed the momentum. I trot backward. I try to catch my breath.

These guys run; they take chances. We have to keep thinking. Be part of the defense, keep them from penetrating. And back up the forwards, be there for a safe pass. Be a coach on the field; all four of our forwards—Dusty, Trunk, Joey, Mitchell—will take any opportunity to dribble instead of pass. So yell at them. Make them think, too.

It's still 1–0 at the half, and the pace has been insane since the start. I sit on the bench and suck on an orange, listening to the coach chew out the forwards.

"Dusty," he's saying. "You have to move toward the ball. Don't wait for it to come to you. Trunk: Stop playing kick-and-chase out there. Dribble if you've got room, but make the smart pass, too. And Joey: You're way the hell out of position. You shouldn't be taking throw-ins; let the mid-fielders do that.

"These guys are running you to death. You're lucky it isn't five–zip. Talk to each other, make good passes, and hustle. We're still in the game, but we've got to penetrate their defense."

I take a deep breath and look straight up. The sky's as blue as our jerseys. I look around at my teammates. They need to get psyched again. "Suck it up," I say. "Let's go."

I wave over the other midfielders—Rico and Hernandez—and we huddle up before the second half begins. "The forwards don't get it," I say.

"They're idiots," says Rico. "Joey's brain goes in one direction. He hasn't passed backwards in his life."

"So holler at him," I say. "And at Dusty, too. Keep yelling for the ball. And work with me. We have to keep the pace down, and we have to control the offense. Our guys can't think and dribble at the same time."

Hernandez is just nodding and sniffing. He's got major allergies.

Rico scowls. "They're never in position. That one time Mitchell made a great cross from the corner, and I look up and Joey's over in the corner, too. Like that does a lot of good."

I shake my head. Rico starts laughing all of a sudden. "Joey," he says, shaking his head. "What a meat grinder."

Joey takes the kickoff, sending it to Trunk, who eases it back to me, and I dribble down the field. I pass to Rico. He yells to Trunk and passes it ahead to him. Soccer's like pinball when everything's working, the ball flying from point to point, making a zigzag path down the field.

We're clicking now, one-touch passes moving it toward their goal. But now Joey's got his head down, dribbling into a cluster of red-and-silver jerseys. "Joey!" I yell. "Joey!" But the ball is already lost.

Rico intercepts it before they can cross midfield. He sends it back to me, and I beat one guy and race downfield. I pass it to Hernandez and he returns it. Now I can dribble, four more steps and I'll shoot. But there are blue shirts near the goal: Joey, Trunk, Dusty. I loft it into the box; Trunk gets control. He slides it toward the corner and Joey fires it, high and hard, into the net. It's tied.

I run back, angry, because it should work like that every time. Most of these guys don't have a consistent awareness of anybody but themselves. And we can't beat a good team playing one on eleven.

The pace finally slows as the third quarter winds down, and the fourth is more of the same. Both teams make runs late in the game, but Herbie makes two great saves for us and their defense doesn't let us in there again. So it ends 1–1.

I sit with Rico on the bus on the way back to Sturbridge. "We should have beat those guys," I say.

"If Pelé up there had half a brain," he says, meaning Joey, who's sitting about six seats up.

"He does," I say. "Maybe even five-eighths."

I shake my head. It's frustrating. Joey's fast, opportunistic. He scores goals and gets girls. But I don't want to be like him.

Well, okay, sometimes I do.

An Insider's Guide

There's a dark alley between Shorty's Bar
and Foley's Pizza, on the Main Street
block between 10th and 11th. You can sit
with your back against either wall--the
green-painted cinder blocks of Foley's or
the brick and mortar of Shorty's. The
attraction, besides being out of the wind,
is the music from Shorty's and the pizza
smell from Foley's.

Foley's crust is a little less doughy
than the other places in town, a little
thinner and browner. So it smells toastier.

The jukebox at Shorty's is programmed to
play the same fourteen songs in succession
unless someone actually feeds it a quarter
and chooses something else. Shorty went
to high school sometime in the 1970s, so
you get these old songs, in this order,
over and over, along with the clicking
of the balls on the pool table:

"Ready for Love" Bad Company
"You Ain't Seen Nothing Yet" Bachman-
    Turner Overdrive
"Can't Fight This Feeling" REO
    Speedwagon
"Freefallin'" Tom Petty and the
    Heartbreakers
"Jack and Diane" John Mellencamp

"Every Breath You Take" The Police

"When I'm With You" Sheriff

"Take It Easy" The Eagles

"I Love Your Way" Peter Frampton

"Rainy Days and Mondays" The Carpenters*

"The Devil Went Down to Georgia"
   Charlie Daniels Band

"Heard It in a Love Song" The Marshall
   Tucker Band

"My Way" Frank Sinatra

"Free Bird" Lynyrd Skynyrd

   *(I am not kidding.)

9
NERVES

After practice on Friday Joey comes up to my locker and sits on the bench. "Tonight, right?" he says.

I shrug. "Yeah." Football game. Shannon and Eileen.

"We gotta get moving," he says.

"It's only quarter after five." What the hell is he up to now?

"We're meeting them at six-thirty. And we gotta stop at work."

"Why?"

"Gotta get something."

"The game's not till eight."

"I know."

He takes a sweatshirt out of my locker and stuffs it into his gym bag. I just look at him, but I'm sure he has a reason for needing my shirt.

"You'll see," he says.

We leave the locker room and head down to Main Street, walking quick but not saying anything. "Kenny's got something for us," Joey finally says, and I figure it has to be alcohol, because there's nothing else I could imagine Kenny getting for us that would be of any use.

We go in the back door and Joey peeks into the kitchen. "Carlos here?" he says to Kenny, who's at the broiler, poking at a steak with a big fork.

Kenny shakes his head without taking his eyes off the

meat. He's got a cigarette hanging from his lip, which should have been enough to answer the question. Carlos threatens to fire Kenny at least once a week for smoking when he's making food, so he doesn't do it if he thinks Carlos is around.

I follow Joey into the walk-in and he unzips the gym bag. He reaches behind the giant plastic jars of salad dressing and pulls out two bottles of apple wine. He puts one in each sleeve of my sweatshirt, then carefully rolls up the shirt and puts it back in the bag. Then we leave.

"You better take this," he says as we cross the parking lot, handing me the bag. "My parents would kill me."

Before I can react he starts walking backward in the direction of his house. "Meet me at the bottom of the path at quarter after," he says. "They're gonna meet us up on the cliff." Then he turns and runs off.

So I'm left standing there with the wine, saying to myself that my parents would kill me, too. I'm two blocks from the YMCA, so I head there. I can stash the stuff in my brother's locker until after dinner.

The cliff overlooks Sturbridge from high above. You can drive up from the other side, but the only way up from town is a long twisting path through the woods. It takes about eleven minutes to walk up. I ran it with Tommy every morning this summer in four and a half.

We're halfway up when Joey sticks out his arm, grabbing my shoulder. He nods toward the down side of the hill, where two deer are browsing on the undergrowth. They're bucks—a nice-sized six-point and an average spike. Joey pulls back an imaginary bow and goes, "Sproing." They look up, black eyes on us, still chewing slowly, staring us down. The bigger one snorts, swishes his tail, and takes one leap away, then walks about twenty feet and stops. The smaller buck follows. They stare at us again from deeper cover, and the big one lowers his head, eyes still on us.

"I didn't think bucks hung around together in the fall," I say.

"They ain't in the rut yet," Joey says. "Not entirely. They'll start fighting over the does soon. Choosing their harems." He starts walking again, a little faster than before. I'm lagging behind, so he turns to speak: "The ones with the bigger horns always win."

There's a cleared spot at the top of the hill about the size of a baseball diamond, with two picnic tables and a small parking area behind us. You can see the whole town spread below you.

It's a warm evening. From this height the town's football shape is most evident—it's a flat oval set down between the hills. All around us the hardwoods are showing their colors—rusts and ambers and bright oranges and reds.

So if you imagine a football-shaped town (I'm not saying it's perfectly symmetrical), then the stripe running toward us is the Pocono River, which reaches the bottom of the cliff and makes a hard turn along the edge of town. And the lacing—right down the middle of the ball (the downtown is just three streets wide)—is Church Street, dotted with six different spires. They're all doing well; Christianity is our most important religion, ahead of football and wrestling.

Route 6 curves in and forms the other stripe, with the cinder block factory just beyond it and the football stadium at the far edge, diagonally across from us tonight. We're about 220 feet above town here. The high school is a block over from the stadium, on the first rise of the hill on that side. That side of the hill climbs as high as over here, though not quite as steeply.

We're sitting on the rim of the bowl up here, with the steepest drop right below us. There's a low wooden snow fence, but it's easy to clear. You'd die if you fell. Or at least you'd get seriously mangled.

Shannon and Eileen aren't here yet (I don't know why we didn't meet at the bottom and walk up with them; that's how I would have done it), so we scout around for a good place to drink. You can't do it out in the open, because the cops sometimes ride up here, especially on nights when there are likely to be parties.

Technically this is a town park, in honor of somebody who donated the land for it, but the only real indication of that is a memorial stone and the Christmas star display, which they light up after Thanksgiving. It gives a pretty cool effect; it's like forty feet tall, so you can see it from everywhere.

Since this is such a small town, there isn't a whole lot of mystery about girls you've gone to school with your whole life. But Shannon and Eileen went to Immaculate Heart through eighth grade, so our paths haven't crossed much. All I know about Eileen is that she plays field hockey and has kind of a pug nose and red hair. Shannon is a gymnast and a hurdler, and I guess you'd say she's willowy.

"Looking good," Joey says suddenly, gazing toward the path,

at the grand entrance. Shannon's a head taller than Eileen, a lot narrower at the hips, and is the only one of the two that is not sweating heavily. She's smiling at us as they approach.

"Nice night," Shannon says as they reach us.

"Easy for you to say," says Eileen. "You just glide up that hill like it's nothing." She opens her mouth wide and hangs out her tongue. She's got a sleeveless yellow shirt on so she has easy access to her armpits, one of which she wipes with the palm of her hand. She sniffs the palm and wipes it on her jeans. "So where are the refreshments?" she says.

"Follow me," says Joey. He starts walking across the grass. There are some big rocks on the side, and you can climb down easy and get out of sight. There's some broken glass—it's not like we're the first to ever drink up here—but the park's mostly clean.

"Would you ladies care for a view of the town?" Joey says. "Or a cozier spot beneath the pines?"

They both laugh. "I want to see my house," Eileen says. "I haven't been up here in years."

So we sit partway down the rocks and Joey opens one of the bottles and takes a swig. He passes it to Shannon, who hands it to Eileen, and then it reaches me.

"Hey, I can see Herbie's bench," Joey says.

"Herbie, too," I say.

"No, it ain't."

"Yes, it is," I say.

"You can't tell."

"Who else sits there?" I ask. There's definitely a guy on the bench, and it sure looks like Herbie from here. What are we, five hundred yards away? "It's Herbie."

"It's Herbie," says Eileen, squinting into the distance. "His shirt says I Am a Macho Stud."

"He's got a new zit on his chin," says Shannon. "And there's a speck of tomato sauce or something on his lip."

I reach for the bottle again. "Believe me, it's Herbie."

"Hi, Herbie," Shannon says, waving in his direction. "Come on up."

When she waves you see the individual muscles in her forearm, lean and sinewy. She brushes her hair back behind her ear and catches me staring at her. She smiles and flicks up her eyebrows. She's sitting cross-legged, slightly above me to my left, with a denim jacket tied around her waist. Eileen is on my level, facing me, but closer to Shannon. Joey is next to her, squinting out toward town.

"That *is* Herbie," Joey says after a few more minutes, and we all laugh.

By seven o'clock there's a definite momentum downtown toward the stadium. More cars are moving that way than the other, and people in the streets are heading there, too. It's getting dark and the streetlights have come on. We'll have to get off the hill soon or we'll have a hell of a time getting down.

There's an inch or two left in one of the bottles and I'm feeling pretty good. The buzz will hit when we stand.

"How many points we get for this?" I ask Joey. This is an ongoing discussion we've been having about how to be cool, how to earn a place among the elite.

"A few," he says. "So far."

"What points?" Eileen asks.

"Status points," I say. "Unofficial."

"You mean like what level you're on? What clique?"

"Like that. Yeah."

Eileen laughs. "You give yourself points for going out with me?"

I blush and laugh and shake my head. "Yeah. . . . I don't know. But you know what I mean. People do keep score. Maybe not with points exactly . . ."

Shannon sits up real straight and smiles. "I think Joey's worth at least a half a point for me," she says. "What do you think, Eileen?"

"Maybe three-quarters. What about Bones? I get any points for being with him?"

"I'd give you one," Shannon tells her. "Two if he tries to make out with you later. . . . Five if you let him."

Not likely. I try to turn this back to a more serious discussion. "You know what I mean. It used to be—like when our parents were in school—being in sports was the coolest thing you could do. Now the coolest people aren't even into sports. If you're in a heavy-metal band or you deal drugs and carry a weapon you're way up there."

"True," Eileen says. "Or if you're screwing some older guy."

Me and Joey turn our heads slowly toward Shannon, then look away fast.

"You guys," she says. "Filthy minds." Then she laughs and reaches for the bottle, and we all watch her drain it.

It got noticeably cooler as the sun went down. Eileen picks up my sweatshirt, the one that had the bottles wrapped in it, and asks if she can wear it. "That's not real clean," I say.

"It won't kill me," she says, pulling it down over her head. The shirt says *Sturbridge Soccer*, and since she doesn't play, but I do, I get a little uneasy about how that will look at the game. But I let it go.

Shannon stands up and puts on her jacket, and we all start heading toward the path. I'll come back for the gym bag tomorrow.

You run the gauntlet of most of the school on your way from the ticket booth to the bleachers. Joey and Shannon are holding hands, with Eileen on one side of them and me on the other, but I can tell people are looking at us as if me and Eileen are together. Which I suppose we are.

I want to get to the bleachers, to be inconspicuous, but Joey leads Shannon toward the refreshment stand, where everybody from our team is hanging. Herbie and some others are over on the dark side, near the bathrooms. Herbie's leaning against the building with a cigarette in his mouth, and Rico and Trunk and Hernandez are there, too.

"Were you on your bench before?" Shannon asks Herbie.

"Of course," he says.

"Like an hour ago?" she asks.

"Probably. How come?"

"Told you," I say.

"We were up on the hill," Shannon says.

"I know."

"You could see us?" she asks.

"I could pick you out a mile away, beautiful."

She blushes and laughs. Herbie, too.

Rico and Trunk and Hernandez are staring at Shannon,

who's got two fingers through one of Joey's belt loops. Eileen pulls on Shannon's arm and says, "Let's hit the bathroom."

They walk away without saying anything.

"What'd you guys drink?" Herbie asks.

"Wine," Joey says. "Guy at work got it for us."

"You get them drunk?"

"Think so," Joey says. "Hope so."

Herbie turns to me and smirks. I kind of roll my eyes. Rico says something to Hernandez under his breath and they giggle. I glare at them. I didn't hear what they said, but I know what they're talking about. I start to explain about helping Joey and all, but stop after one word. "She's—"; then I say screw it to myself. "I'm going to take a piss," I say, and walk away.

Girls generally take longer in the bathroom than guys, so when I come out they're coming out, too. Shannon puts her arm around my shoulders; that makes me feel sort of warm but also like I'm her little brother or something. My hands are at my sides.

"Let's get munchies," Shannon says.

So we go to the refreshment window and she asks for four Cokes and two lollipops. "Okay, Eileen?" she says, turning to her.

"Yeah. Get me a purple one."

I reach for my wallet, but Shannon says she'll pay. She takes her arm off my shoulders and pulls out her wallet. She takes out four dollars and sets her wallet on the counter.

She picks up two of the Cokes and Eileen takes the others.

"Would you put my wallet in my pocket?" Shannon asks me. She eases her butt toward me, and I slip the wallet into the right back pocket of her jeans, which is a tight squeeze. I do it as carefully as possible. Eileen smiles and shakes her head. Then we walk back to where Joey and the others are.

We sit about fifteen rows up at the forty-yard line: Joey-Shannon-me-Eileen.

We fall behind early, but Lenny Olver takes a pitchout in the second quarter and goes forty-eight yards with it, tying the score. The band breaks into "Born to Run" and the cheerleaders do a kind of sexy dance.

I nudge Shannon.

"Why aren't you down there?"

"Cheering?"

"Yeah."

She shakes her head. "I'm too flat."

I tilt my head and look closer, and she puts her hand in my face and her other arm over her chest. But she's laughing.

I give her a look that lets her know what an outrageous statement she's made, but she clicks her tongue and says, "Well, I am."

I look past her at Joey, who's squinting toward the field. He can't see worth a damn without his glasses. Maybe he can't hear, either, because he hasn't said anything since we sat down. He's just there. In my way.

After the game Shannon and Joey disappear, so me and Eileen walk slowly toward her house. I know where it is because she pointed it out from the cliff. We walk along

Maple, which is a block above Main and is quiet and dark. There's no sidewalk here, so we walk in the street.

I don't know what to do with my hands. We don't say anything, but she keeps looking over at me as we walk.

"Pretty good game," I say after we've gone three blocks.

She lets out her breath. "Yeah."

We walk another block, and then my hand brushes hers by mistake. "Oh," she says.

I stick my hand in my pocket. She stops suddenly and steps to the side of the road and bends over.

"What are you doing?" I say.

Then she pukes. Not much gagging, just a couple of quick wet heaves.

I step back and look away. "You all right?" I ask.

She walks back a few feet and doesn't answer. I hear her say "Shit" to herself. She wipes her mouth with her sleeve, which of course is really *my* sleeve.

After a minute we start walking again.

"You make me really nervous," she says finally.

"I do?"

"Uh-huh."

"How come?"

"I don't know," she says. "I mean, you're out with me, but I don't exactly seem like your first choice."

"Oh."

"You never take your eyes off her."

I start scratching my jaw. "No?" I stop walking. "Sorry," I say.

She shrugs. "It's okay. Sometimes I can't stop looking at her, either."

We come down from Maple toward Main. She lives near

the river, on Court Street. We cross Main a block up from Herbie's bench, which is already occupied. When we're about a half block in from Main, I hear somebody, sounds like Hernandez, shout, "Go for it, Bones!"

I pretend not to hear. So does she. But Hernandez is due for some sharp elbows at practice next week.

"You feeling okay?" I ask, the first thing I've said in a few minutes.

"Yeah," she says, slowly drawing out the word, like a sigh. She laughs once, almost like a huff of air coming out. "I have a knack for graceful performances like that."

"Me, too," I say.

"Yeah? Like what?"

I stop walking and put my foot up on this low cement wall in front of a house. "I was in this play in kindergarten. It was a third-grade play, but they needed some little kids to be stuffed clowns in a toy shop. The toys came to life at night when the shop was closed. So me and two girls from kindergarten got to be in the play. Mostly we just sat there, but in one scene we got to do somersaults and stuff."

I catch my breath. She sits on the wall about two feet from my shoe. "So I do a somersault and bang my nose on the floor, and blood starts gushing out. They had to stop the play for a while, then they just pulled me off the stage and finished without me."

"Sounds cute," she says.

"My mother thought so."

"I've thrown up in school twice," she says. "Once on the playground in kindergarten and once in seventh grade. All over my desk. Never even felt it coming."

"Hit anybody else?"

"The girl in front of me, a little. Mr. DiPalma just threw a handful of that green stuff on it."

"Magic Puke-Away."

"Yeah. But what stunk was that the nurse wouldn't even let me go home. I sat in her office for like two hours."

"You ever wet your pants?" I ask.

Her eyes get wider. "Nice question."

"I did. Not in school, but at a track meet. In first grade."

"I'm not sure I want to hear this one." But she's smiling and leaning toward me. I sit down.

"It was the Y program. There were more than a hundred kids in it, so there's twenty heats or so in the hundred meters, and I'm in the eighteenth one. And it's cool and drizzly, and I'm nervous because this is my first real race. And we finally get to the starting line and get down in our starting position, and I focus on the track ahead of me. The starter goes 'Take your marks,' and I stretch out my legs and set my fingers down at the line. 'Set . . .' and I raise up on my fingers and lift my butt, and I feel this warmth spreading over my crotch, and hear this tinkling sound hitting the track. And the starter starts laughing, and he walks over to me and squats down. He's real nice about it. He just says, 'There's a bathroom in that building near the finish line,' and he pats me on the head.

"Then we go, and I win the race and keep going, right into the bathroom. Which doesn't really make a lot of sense, since I've already gone. So I just pull my shirt out of my shorts and stretch it as low as it goes. But I have to do the long jump next, and the sand sticks to my wet shorts."

We both crack up. Then we stop. I stop because it dawns

on me that we're sitting here in the dark on this cement wall, me and her. And I remember Shannon's remark about making out. And Hernandez's crack about going for it. We both move our heads about an eighth of a turn and look at each other, then turn back a quarter turn. I start chewing on my lip. She starts bouncing her knee up and down.

We're quiet for a few minutes, then she says she'd better get in.

"Okay." We start walking again.

"I'll wash your sweatshirt," she says.

"Thanks. No hurry."

We don't go up her walk, but hang back in the shadows of the driveway, in the partial light from the porch. And her eyes look sort of scared, or maybe defiant, and her coarse red hair has an electric, shampooed sheen. I inch closer, and she turns her lips toward me, her mouth curling slightly at the corner in a sneer or a twitch or an invitation.

My voice cracks, but I find it, halting my approach for a second. Out comes my half-whispered plea: "Let's see if you taste like puke." And she doesn't; only the hint of a Cert she must have slipped in there.

I back away, nodding and sputtering a good-night.

" 'Night," she says, watching me go. Finally I turn with a quick, jerky wave, then walk away in a hurry and don't look back.

Her lips were moist and firm, surprisingly pleasant for someone with such a nervous stomach.

That was an okay evening.

But this is getting me nowhere.

10
THE MENTAL COURT

Saturday is one of the rare nights when the whole family eats together, so Mom makes a big deal of it. She and Dad have wine with dinner, and we eat in the dining room instead of the kitchen.

We sit down for roast beef, and Dad asks Tommy if he got any letters today.

"Two," he answers. "Bucknell and some little school in Maine." Tommy has only wrestled two years, but he gets like ten letters a week from colleges trying to recruit him. Part of that comes from the program he's in—Sturbridge has been nationally ranked the past two seasons. Two guys won state titles in back-to-back weight classes a couple of years ago, and that put us on the map, big-time.

"We'll need to make some visits soon, to help you get an idea of what these schools are like," says Mom. "A big school like Penn State or Rutgers is like a city in itself. You might be more at home on a smaller campus."

My parents went to Lycoming College, out by Williamsport, and they'd like nothing better than for Tommy and me to go there, too. But Lycoming doesn't offer athletic scholarships, and Tommy's drive is big enough that he's wanting to join a major program. I'm guessing it'll be Penn State, because that's where the two guys who won the states two years ago went. Everybody's counting on Tommy to win it this year and next.

"What about you, Barry?" my father asks, turning to me. "Do anything good in practice today?"

"Usual stuff," I say. "Ran a lot."

My mother puts her hand on my shoulder. "That Donna Luther was running the register when I checked out at the supermarket this afternoon," she says. "She's a real cutie."

"Is she?" I say, meaning I don't think so. She's cute only by a mother's criteria, meaning attractive in a way that ensures that nothing physical might happen. This is my mother's way of figuring out if I'm normal, though. Drop names of girls she thinks are safe and gauge my reaction.

Mom's a loan officer at the bank. Dad sells insurance. Pretty boring jobs, but we're better off than most of my friends. This is Mom's town: she grew up here and knows everybody and was Miss Popular all through school. Dad grew up here, too, but he seems a step or two out of touch. He's two years older, and they hardly knew each other before college.

My parents get to some of my soccer games and track meets. They get to all of the wrestling matches, and most of Tommy's cross-country races even though he's only like sixth man on the JV. But I ain't jealous. I couldn't hate my brother if I tried.

When I get up to leave my mother asks, "Going to Joey's?" She never used to even ask. For about eight years it was understood that if I left the house I was going to Joey's, and if he left his house he was coming over here. Now she figures she has to ask, because she's beginning to sense that there's more to my world than Joey's house. She's just not sure what.

I shrug and say maybe. But I haven't been to Joey's in weeks. I like being on Main Street, but I do miss just hanging in my room or Joey's once in a while and listening to music or playing chess. Talking about life. About girls. About sex—not how to do it, but whether we'd do it, or when. Now he's moving in that direction and I'm right where I've always been.

I walk up to Main Street. Herbie's eating a hot dog from Turkey Hill, and Rico's there, too, chewing gum. Rico's only been hanging with us a few weeks. He moved here from Jersey City in the middle of our freshman year and hardly said a word to anybody until this season started.

"You're late," Herbie says, thrusting a finger at me. "We missed three prime candidates because of your tardiness."

"Sorry," I say. "Had to meet my weekly boredom quotient at home."

"Inexcusable," he says.

"They'll be back," I say. The count is sixty-three, and the pace hasn't slowed much.

"So how'd the big date go?" Herbie asks. He and Rico are smirking, like they already know all about it.

"Okay, I guess."

"I heard she said hello to Ralph." They both crack up. I hadn't said a word to anybody about her puking. She must have told Shannon. Shannon must have told Joey. Joey must have told everybody that would listen.

"Yeah." I admit it.

"I like that in a girl," Herbie says. "It's attractive."

"Eat shit," I say, but I'm starting to laugh, too. Mostly from embarrassment.

"It sets the mood," Herbie says. "Lets you know she really likes you."

Rico is just giggling his ass off, not able to say anything. Finally he sputters out, "Was there any ham in it?"

"Ham?"

"Little chunks of ham. Or string beans."

"I didn't examine it." Actually I did run by that spot this morning when I was doing my roadwork, but I won't tell them that. "I think it was mostly wine and soda," I say. "It didn't sound . . . solid."

We stare at the cars going by for a few minutes. Herbie says "Sixty-four" when Mr. Torcelli, a whiny algebra teacher, drives by.

"Know where Joey is?" I ask.

"Him and Dusty went over to the Mental Court," Rico says.

The Mental Court is at the end of Church Street, by the river. There's a group home there, not for delinquents, but for odd people. They're autistic or schizoid or something. Anyway, there's a basketball court there, and it's open all the time and has lights.

I don't really want to see Joey, I just wanted to know where he was. Who he was with. He's playing basketball with Dusty. I'm okay with that.

On Tuesday we get hammered by Scranton Prep. It's not a league game, but it shows there's still a gap between us and the really good teams in the area. It was 3–1, but they dominated.

After the game me and Joey head for work. We're

exhausted from the game and the bus ride and don't feel like working tonight.

As we're leaving the locker room Joey says, "You played really good, but they kicked our butts."

"Yeah. They got a lot of experience."

"They work at it," he says. "Too many of our guys are only into it in the fall."

It's true. Me and Joey work on foot skills and passing all year, but most of our players forget soccer as soon as the season ends.

"You were the best player out there," I say.

He considers this, then shakes his head. "They had two better guys. Number Eight and that little midfielder."

"I guess, maybe."

"They were," he says. "Next year we'll be at that level. In two years we'll be a powerhouse. We've just got to get the rest of our guys to commit more. They've got to want it like we do."

About nine we're loading up the dishwasher, and Joey points out that Kenny's asleep in the office. It's a slow night, hardly any customers. "We could get some stuff," he says.

"Like what?"

"Whatever. Steaks or something."

"What would we do with them?"

"I don't know," he says. "Take 'em home and eat 'em."

"Are your parents home?"

"Yeah."

"Well, we ain't cooking them at my house," I say.

"Yeah. Maybe we could stash them somewhere until the weekend."

"Like under a rock somewhere?"

"I don't know."

"They have to be refrigerated," I say.

"Oh, yeah."

He starts going through the silverware, tossing some heavily crusted pieces into the trash can. "Maybe we can get a cooler with some ice and hide it in my garage," he says. "Maybe next week."

Maybe. "We'll see," I say.

"We could have a hell of a good party," he says. "I bet we could get enough for ten people."

"I suppose."

"Find out if your parents are going away anytime soon," he says. "This could turn out great."

▌▌
HAIRCUT

Coach lets us out early on Wednesday, so I walk down the hill to get a haircut. I go to Jerry's because it's only six bucks; I'm not spending fourteen to have it "designed" somewhere else.

All three barbers are busy, so I take a seat in one of those red-vinyl-covered chairs with shiny metal arms. The barbers are all brothers in their fifties; I think Jerry was their father. They never say much to kids except to ask you how short you want it. They're wearing matching maroon barber shirts, and their hair is so slick you can see every furrow made by the comb teeth.

My father says this place hasn't changed one bit since he was a kid, and probably not for a lot longer than that. They've got a radio station from New Jersey (how do they get it? I've never once heard it at home, and I flip through the stations constantly) playing big band stuff from the thirties and forties.

One guy finishes and waves me over, and I take the chair. "Regular cut?" he asks.

That's a dangerous question, because regular is relative, but I say, "Yeah. Not too short, though."

He goes to work. The door opens and I'm surprised because Footstepper walks in. I'm in the chair closest to the door, and the guy cutting my hair says, "What's the good word, Jack?"

Footstepper blushes and says, "Hello, Gene." The other two barbers say hello, too, and he nods. Then he goes in the back and comes out with a broom. He starts sweeping the floor, creating big piles of hair. He makes three piles, one from around each chair, taking great care to keep the three separate. He sweeps the three piles, one at a time, toward the back, but then uses a dustpan to dump each of the piles into the same trash can.

When he's done with that he goes into the bathroom and starts mopping the floor. The floor is foot-square green and cream tiles, and he seems to be mopping each one individually, carefully staying within each square until it's done. I can see this because he leaves the door open. He's still at it when I pay for the haircut and head for home.

It's not dark yet, and I've got a lot of energy. Practice was easy. I head down toward Court Street and start jogging. I feel like moving.

I reach the river and turn back up toward Main, crossing the bridge and running faster. I pass the Y and cut across a yard to get to the path that heads up to the cliff.

I get up it fast—probably under four minutes to the top. I stop to catch my breath, sweating under my clothes.

I lean against the fence and look out at the town. It's steep here—I'm twenty feet above the tops of the highest level of maples. I can hear a truck shifting gears. A shout but not the words. Dogs barking, a car door slamming. But they're all in the distance, just background sounds way below me.

I can see our house, gray with a darker gray roof. Most of the roofs are shades of gray, light to black. The houses are white, gray, blue, with window trim and doors of brown and forest green. A few of the houses are brick red, but not brick. The only brick buildings are the churches, the courthouse, and the Y.

Our yards are small on this end of town, and well trodden. I can make out the base paths on Hernandez's back lawn.

It's a town of clustered squares, with steep roofs and gray chimneys. I think it's a good place to grow up. But I'm not sure what happens after that. It seems like a hard town to stay in. Maybe it's nice to come back to, though.

I decide to walk down, because I've done the work and it's starting to get dark now. I'm definitely late for dinner.

12
HOME

"We suck," Herbie says as we walk off the field. Me, Herbie, and Rico are trailing behind the others. We're pissed off because we should have won this game, but we only managed a scoreless tie. I'm grumbling about Joey hogging the ball. Herbie says he cost us the win. Joey does all this talking about bringing the other players up to our level, but when game time comes he still tries to be a one-man team.

Wallenpaupack's not in our league, so it doesn't matter a whole lot, but we still should have beat them. Next week we start the second half of the league schedule, playing each team again, and we needed a win to gain some momentum.

Herbie yells toward the group walking ahead of us. "Hey, Joey," he says. "Some of us were wondering. You've been playing soccer a long time. Did you ever have an assist?"

Joey turns and starts to speak, then realizes that Herbie's busting his chops. "Screw you, Herbie," he says.

"No, I mean it."

"I had one last week."

"Oh, yeah. I forgot about that. I thought you just lost control of the ball that time."

Joey squints and stares at Herbie. He had at least three opportunities to set up goals today—he could have fed me twice—but he tried to take it in on his own every time. "I don't think so," he says.

Herbie says to me and Rico, "I figured he must have had one somewhere along the line."

Joey stops and takes a step toward us. "What'd you say?"

Herbie keeps walking. "I said I figured you must have had one sometime in your career."

"You got a problem, pal?"

Herbie stops and faces Joey. He's got a smile on his face and I don't think he's looking for a fight. He knows how to get to Joey, though. "No problem. Just curious."

"Screw you," Joey says again.

"I just wondered, you know, with all your talent, if you ever tried to spread it around," Herbie says. "You know, actually pass the ball instead of barging through people."

"I got nine goals this year," Joey says.

Herbie nods. He's still grinning. "And one assist."

"Yeah."

"Just making sure I've got the count right."

"You got it right."

"Pretty good ratio," Herbie says.

"I'd say so."

Dusty has come over now, and most of the team is gathering around. "What's your point, Herbie?" he says. Dusty plays forward, too, so he probably feels under attack.

"No point. Just thinking how much better we might be if we had an offense instead of a star."

"Maybe you just wish you were the star, huh?"

"Maybe," Herbie says. "Maybe not."

Joey chimes in again. "There's a reason we play offense, you know."

"Yeah?"

"You think you get stuck playing goalie because you're a good soccer player?"

Joey's getting pissed, and Herbie can sense it. He'll keep it up until Joey either starts swinging or walks away. I'm enjoying it—Joey deserves this—but I notice Coach walking toward us from the bus.

Joey makes another stupid-ass comment about the good athletes playing up front. "I'd like to see you run like we do, cigarette man," he says to Herbie.

Herbie puts his hands over his heart and staggers backward. "God, what biting sarcasm," he says. "I can't take it."

"Right, loser. You can't."

Coach has reached us now, but he doesn't say anything. He just looks at Herbie, then at Joey, then at me. "Everybody get on the bus," he finally says. "Except you, Herbie."

We walk slowly to the bus; I can hear Coach yelling at Herbie about acting stupid. Joey's glaring at me hard. I glare back.

"Nice new friend you got," he says.

I just look away. Aren't I allowed to have more than one friend? I take a seat by a window next to Rico and nobody says anything. We just look out at Coach and Herbie, back on the field. Herbie starts running laps. Coach walks over and gets on the bus and stares straight ahead. Herbie does five laps around the field, then walks to the bus, takes his time getting on, and sits in the seat in front of me. He turns and gives me a big grin as the bus pulls out of the parking lot.

Saturday night we all meet at Herbie's bench—Rico, me, Hernandez, Herbie. The count is at seventy-six, but it's slowed down considerably. The town has yielded most of its regulars already; the final candidates will be surprises.

It's a dull night. There's a party going on somewhere, but it's mostly juniors and seniors. After a while Rico and Hernandez decide to walk over to the Mental Court for some hoops.

So it's 10:30 and just me and Herbie are sitting there.

"Too early to go home," I say.

"It's always too early for that," he says.

I say yeah, but then I start thinking about it. If I did go home I'd probably watch TV with my parents or hang in my room and read. It would be even duller than sitting here on the bench, but it wouldn't be horrible. I get the feeling that it wouldn't be quite the same at Herbie's house.

"You ever go home?" I ask.

He gives me a puzzled look. "What, are you kidding?"

"No."

"Yeah, I go home."

I nod.

He sticks a cigarette between his lips and starts digging in his coat pocket for his lighter. "I try to see Pete as little as I can," he says. Pete is his father.

"Yeah." His father beats him up sometimes. Maybe his mother, too.

He gets the cigarette lit and blows a bluish stream of smoke straight up. "He's a fine man."

I just nod some more. Part of me wishes I could say I know how it is, say that my father is a son of a bitch, too, that he's bitter and that he cuts me down and slaps me around and thinks I'm a loser. But none of that is true. Not in my case.

A car pulls up in front of the bench and stops. It's my parents' car, but Tommy is driving. Tony Terranova rolls down the passenger window and says, "Gentlemen."

"Tony," I say.

"Hi, guys," says Shannon, who's sitting between Tony and my brother in the front seat. She leans across Tony and says, "Seen Joey?"

"Hours ago," I say. "I thought he was with you."

"He was supposed to show up at Debbie's," she says. That's the party house. Obviously Joey never got there. I don't think Shannon's all that distressed about it.

My brother gets out of the driver's side, but the car is still running. He comes over to the bench. "What's going on?" he says. He shakes hands with Herbie, who he hardly knows.

"Nothing," I answer. "Party any good?"

"For a little while," he says, gazing down Main Street. "I wasn't into it."

He notices that I'm looking at the car, trying to assess what's going on with Shannon. Tommy turns to look at Turkey Hill, so he's not facing the car, and he motions with his head for me to come around the other side of him.

"We're just giving her a ride home," he says quietly. "You wanna come?"

I shrug. "I guess." I turn toward the bench and say, "Herbie, wanna get off that bench and cruise around a little?"

"Gee, I dunno," he says. "It might throw off the balance of the universe if I abandon this spot." He gets up, though, and reaches for the back door handle. He and I get into the backseat, and Tommy pulls onto the street.

We do a few loops of the town, not saying a whole lot. Shannon turns around and leans toward Herbie, slapping him on the knee. "Heard you and Joey almost got into it the other day," she says, smiling.

"No big deal," Herbie says. He puts up his fists and kind of rolls them around. "Just a little sparring, you know. A manly exchange of words."

"Yeah, so I heard."

"Just parrying back and forth," Herbie says. "Two worthy opponents."

She's kneeling on the front seat now, turned completely toward us. She shakes her head and laughs. "You crack me up."

We wind up driving all the way to Weston and back, just for the hell of it. We get doughnuts. It's about 11:45 when we drop her off. Herbie gets out on Main Street and we drop Tony at his house. Then me and Tommy head for home.

"Nice girl," he says after we've gone about two blocks.

"She's fantastic," I say, immediately wishing I hadn't.

He smirks a little and nods slowly. His smile gets a little bigger.

"Shit," I say, just to myself. Tommy punches me on the arm and turns up our street. But when we get to the house he keeps going.

He turns toward River Road and makes a left, past the cemetery and up the hill into farm country. "You gonna ask her out sometime?" he says.

I shrug. "She's kind of . . . I don't know. Joey's like . . . you know."

He tilts his head back and forth. "Joey didn't even show up tonight," he says.

"Did that piss her off?"

"Didn't seem to." Tommy looks like he's thinking hard. "Remember when I was a freshman and I had to beat Tony to make the varsity?" he asks.

"Yeah."

"I did beat him. He didn't like it, but we stayed friends," he says. "Better friends, even."

I see the point he's trying to make, but I don't agree with it. "I think that's different," I say slowly.

He's quiet for a moment. "Yeah," he says. "It is."

"She's over my head anyway."

"Is she?"

"I think so," I say. "The thing is, she ought to be over Joey's head, too."

"You're probably right. Thing is, Joey doesn't think so." He starts drumming with his fingers on the steering wheel. "Then again, maybe he does."

I nod. Tommy pulls into a driveway and turns the car around. We don't say much the rest of the way, but I feel okay. Not about Shannon, but about myself. Tommy doesn't have all the answers, but he has more than I do. He sees my situation more clearly than I can.

You need people like that in your life.

An Insider's Guide

Some night if you can't sleep, get up
and take a walk at three o'clock in the
morning. Sneak out of the house without
making a sound, and stick to back
streets so you can duck into the shadows
when a cop car goes by. Here are some
things you might see if you stay out for
an hour:

- Two doctors in green scrubs standing
  on the loading dock outside the
  hospital's emergency room, smoking
  cigarettes.
- The skinny guy with funny teeth who
  runs the Chinese takeout place,
  in the driveway behind his
  restaurant, hosing down cabbages.
- Night-shift guys at Sturbridge
  Building Products, taking a coffee
  break in the parking lot.
- A prominent attorney walking an
  incontinent dog.
- Me.

13
ELEVEN MUSKETEERS

We figured we'd start off the second half of the season in a big way, trashing Weston North on our home field. There's a few dozen people here to cheer us on. And we shut these guys out last month.

But the first quarter's almost over and we've barely crossed midfield. North is putting on some pressure. Their right wing is dribbling toward me, and I attack. He crosses it to another forward, who takes a long shot that Herbie catches. Herbie looks downfield, but heaves it over to my side. I'm shielded by that same wing, and he gets control and starts cutting in from the sideline, a step ahead of me, bearing down on the goal. I catch up and go into a slide tackle, but he steps on the ball and stops short, and I'm on the ground and he's past me. He chips it toward the center, and their striker heads it into the goal.

Dusty bumps into me as he jogs back into position. "What the hell kind of a tackle was that?" he says.

I stare at him. "It's called defense."

"It is, huh?"

"Eat shit." See if I pass to him later.

Herbie calls over the defenders and the midfielders at the end of the quarter. "Tighten up," he says. "They've had six shots on goal already."

"We're overcommitting on defense," Rico says. "Don't challenge if you can't win the ball. Hold your ground."

"And clear the friggin' ball," Herbie says. "At least twice we made little girlie passes right in front of our net that could have cost us."

Coach yells for us to line up for the kickoff. Rico trots next to me as we head downfield. "That Dusty's one hell of a guy, huh?"

I sneer. "Yeah."

"Joey, too," he says. "They're two one hell of a guys."

Second quarter starts out okay. We get the ball down into their end, at least. Trunk tries to pass it through one of their midfielders, and it gets deflected out of bounds. I race over and grab the ball for a throw-in. Dusty's got room ahead of me, but I throw it short, back to Rico. He slides it to me, and I dribble downfield. I could pass, but I don't, moving the ball up the touchline.

I race past the wing who beat me before, but a midfielder comes up and taps the ball out of bounds. I scoop it up and throw it down the line, where Mitchell controls it and pokes it toward the center. Joey gets it, dribbles twice, and takes a shot from too far out. It bounces off a defender on my side and I race to control it. I'm out of position, but I've got the ball and an open path to the goal.

I'm sprinting now, racing with the ball, but a wall of three defenders is closing in, squeezing me toward the corner. I stop, do a full turn, and penetrate toward the center. I hear them yelling for the ball—Dusty, Trunk, Joey—but now I'm surrounded. I can't shoot or pass.

They clear it out of there, and suddenly the ball and three North forwards are way the hell ahead of us, streaking toward our goal. Three quick passes and it's in our penalty area. Hernandez falls down, Herbie cuts toward the ball, and a softly rolling grounder squeaks past him and crosses the goal mouth.

They've got a guy waiting, he taps it home. He's offside, but it doesn't get called. It's 2–0 and Joey and Dusty are both in my face this time.

"What the hell was that?" Joey says.

"Penetration," I say.

"You ever hear of passing?" Dusty shouts at me.

"Yeah. But I didn't know you had."

Joey grabs Dusty's arm and leads him away. Then he turns to me. "Suck it up," he says.

I let out my breath and nod.

Joey comes over and punches me lightly on the arm. "Good hustle," he says. "Keep it up."

Coach chews us out good at the half. We haven't made a meaningful pass the whole game and we've made some blatantly stupid defensive errors.

I haven't played this badly since I was about nine.

As we're walking back onto the field Joey comes up beside me. "What gives, man?" he says.

"Don't know."

"You gotta get me the ball."

I nod. "And you gotta give it up sometimes."

"Right. Now let's get this done." He claps his hands and starts jogging. "Let's get it done!" he shouts.

But we never do get it together. Joey manages to score late

in the third off a corner kick, but North gets it right back. We lose 3–1 and walk off the field shaking our heads.

"This sucks," Dusty says to no one in particular, although he's looking my way. But he keeps walking. I slow down and drift into a pack with Hernandez and Herbie.

"You know what's really great about this team?" Herbie says after a minute. "Our sense of unity. The way we're all pulling together."

I'm still pissed, but I can't help but smile.

"Total, unselfish dedication to the cause," he says. "Eleven Musketeers."

"It sure is great," I say, looking around as my teammates trudge toward the locker room with their heads down.

"It's a special kind of wonderful," Herbie says, and I burst out laughing.

We've reached the locker room and Coach is waiting in the doorway. "What the hell is wrong with you?" he asks. "We just got our butts whipped and you guys think it's funny?"

I turn solemn. "I wasn't laughing about that," I say.

"You shouldn't be laughing at all," he says to me. Then he turns and addresses the whole team. "You guys were pathetic out there today," he says, pushing the door shut with his foot. "What kind of a team is this?" His voice is getting louder. "I don't know what's going on, but you're turning this season to shit. We've got two factions here— you know who you are—and they're working against each other. If you can't straighten it out, then the JV guys will move up and take your places."

He lets out his breath and slams his fist into a locker—

not too hard, just to make a point. "Whatever's going on, whatever personality conflicts you may have off the field, I expect you to leave it behind you when you step into your soccer uniforms. If you can't do that, then you've got no business being on this team. Bones. Joey. Dusty. Whoever else is involved in this—I'll bench your ass real fast if you play another minute the way you played today."

He turns and leaves the locker room, and we all sit there in silence. Mitchell is the only senior on the team and he's the captain, but he's just staring at the floor. Joey's got his arms folded and he's glaring at Herbie. Herbie raises his eyebrows at him, like he's waiting for him to speak. Joey just says "Asshole" under his breath.

"That's helpful," I say.

"I wasn't talking to you," he says.

"I know."

"I was talking to your girlfriend."

That's so stupid that I just look away. Dusty stands and says, "Everybody shut up." He steps out into the center of the room and looks around at us. He points a finger at Rico, then at me. "You guys aren't getting us the ball."

"You guys don't know what to do with it," I say.

"Bullshit," he says. "You don't wanna admit that we're the reason this team is winning."

"Guess what, pal. We haven't won a game in two weeks."

"Guess what, yourself. That's when you stopped playing like a team."

Other guys start shouting now, throwing in their two cents. After a couple of minutes Coach sticks his head in and yells, "Shut up!" The room turns deadly quiet. "Every one of you," he says in a steady, angry voice, "get showered, get dressed, and get the hell out of here. When I see you tomorrow you'd better be ready to run." He looks around the room for effect. "And you'd better be ready to act like a team. Or you won't be one anymore."

14

THE METHODIST POPE

We get no warm-up at practice today, no jogging or dribbling drills or juggling. Coach just tells us to line up across the goal line. Then we run line drills—sprinting to the eighteen-yard line, turning and sprinting back to the goal line, then up to midfield, back to the eighteen, down to the opposite eighteen, back to midfield, down to the far goal line, then all the way back to where we started.

"You've got thirty seconds to relax," he says. "Enjoy it."

We're all bent over, hands on our knees, gasping for breath. Then he blows his whistle and we do it again, with him shouting at us to quit dogging it.

We do the whole routine eight times, and Trunk and Hernandez both throw up when we finish.

"Herbie," Coach says. "You were last in every one."

"I'm biding my time," Herbie says. He wipes his nose and coughs.

"You're what?"

"Conserving some energy."

"You won't have any energy when I'm through with you," Coach says. "Line up."

Everybody groans. "All of us?" Dusty says.

"No. Just Herbie. The guy who saved so much energy."

Herbie sneers and shakes his head, but he walks up to the line. Coach blows his whistle, and Herbie takes off, maybe a little faster than before.

✹   ✹   ✹

We're late for work, but extra running is really no big deal for me and Joey. We kind of like it.

It's busy tonight, so we're camped out by the dishwasher. We're running a steak-and-shrimp special, so there's a lot of cocktail sauce on the edges of the plates.

My forehead's wet from dishwasher steam and the floor is slippery. But we're in pretty good moods, despite everything.

Joey's hosing down a tray of dishes and he looks over at me. "You talk to Shannon lately?" he asks.

"Not really. I saw her Saturday night. She was looking for you."

"Yeah."

"Yeah. She said you were supposed to show up at that party."

He shoves the tray onto the conveyor belt and starts loading another. "I wasn't up for it."

"No?"

"She messes with my head."

"She does?"

"She's always talking about other guys."

"Really? Like who?"

"Lots of guys. Like your brother, even. And your asshole friend Herbie."

"What does she say?"

He looks up at the ceiling and scratches at his nose. "Like they're cute or funny or whatever," he says.

"Yeah, but you're the one she's with."

"Sometimes. Not that often."

"What do you mean?"

"I see her like once a week."

That's news to me, because I hardly ever see Joey outside of work and soccer anymore. "So you're not . . ." I stop. Not what? "So where do you go every night?" I ask.

"Around."

"Why don't you hang out with us? On Main Street."

He frowns. "I don't like some of the company."

"Oh."

Kenny calls me over and asks me to keep an eye on three steaks he's got under the broiler. "Gotta get something in the walk-in," he says.

He could have just as easily sent me to the walk-in, except that what he needs is a beer. So I grab a fork and flip the steaks and listen to them sizzle until he gets back.

"Find what you needed?" I ask.

Kenny just grunts.

"Cold and frosty?" I say.

He glares at me. I'm just kidding around. Screw him if he can't take a joke.

I return to the dishwashing area, and Joey continues his talk.

"Maybe I really should go into the priesthood," he says. Until about sixth grade he wanted to be a priest, then he started to figure out some of the realities of that profession. So he's not serious, but I humor him.

"I think you have to be at least reasonably smart to be a priest," I say.

"Yeah. But I'm in good with Father Jim."

"Well, maybe he could get you in. But you'd probably never get to be bishop or pope or anything."

"Probably not," he says.

"I wouldn't mind that job, with the big pointy hat."

"You ain't even Catholic."

"Yeah," I say. "But maybe I could, like, be a Methodist pope."

"Yeah, maybe." He smiles and starts fishing the silverware out of the basin.

I stand there a few seconds and look at him. He's okay. Then I head into the back to work on the sinkful of pots.

15
SORTING PENNIES

Friday at dinner my mother announces that we're going away next weekend to look at colleges.

"I got a game on Saturday," I say.

"Well, can't you miss just one?" she says.

"No way."

My father clears his throat. "Is it a morning game?"

"No," I say. "It's at one."

"Hmmm," Dad says. He turns to Mom. "It would hardly be worth going if we waited until after the game."

"Let him stay home," Tommy says. "What's the big deal?"

Mom frowns. "It is a big deal," she says, looking at me. "You've never been alone overnight in this house."

I shrug. "So what? I can't miss that game. Or any game. We could win the league."

She sighs. "We'll see."

Nobody says anything for about a minute. "Where you going?" I ask.

"Well," she says, "we'd planned to go to upstate New York and visit Colgate, Binghamton, and Ithaca. It would be good for you, too, not just for Tommy."

"He'll be all right," Tommy says. "Don't make him miss his game."

"You'll be missing a cross-country race," she says.

"No comparison," he says. "That's not my sport. If it

was a wrestling match there's no way I would miss it. Soccer is his sport."

"Maybe we'd better wait until the season is over," she says.

"Wrestling starts right after soccer," Tommy says. "We gotta go now."

She purses her lips and turns to my father. "Do you have any thoughts on this?" she asks him.

He leans back in his chair and tilts his head from one side to the other, like he's trying to weigh his brain. "I suppose he'd be all right," he finally says.

"Well," Mom says. "We'll see."

I flop down on my bed after dinner and stare at the ceiling. We won a game yesterday, but it didn't feel so great. We beat Mount Ridge 4–2, but they suck. We still aren't playing well. We beat them on skill and aggression, not teamwork.

I can hear my father sorting coins in my parents' room. He's not a collector or anything, but he's got this metal box with four compartments for pennies, nickels, dimes, and quarters, and he keeps it organized.

My mother appears in the doorway. "Well," she says. "I guess it will be all right if you stay home next weekend. But no monkey business. We'll be home Sunday afternoon and the house had better be spotless."

"No problem," I say. "Thanks."

"Well," she says for the eightieth time since dinner, "you know the rules."

My father looks in and winks at me. "Hey, sport," he

says. "Just about time to go?" he asks my mom. They're going over to the mall in Scranton.

"Not quite," she says. "I'm waiting for the washer to finish so I can get those things into the dryer."

"Okay," he says. He's carrying a copy of *Reader's Digest.* "I'll be on the john. Just let me know when you're ready."

He starts whistling as he walks down the hall with the magazine under his arm. Mom heads for the washing machine in the cellar. Tommy's in his room with music playing, not too loud, getting ready to go out. I run a comb through my hair and grab my wallet from my dresser.

Herbie and Rico are the only ones out when I get up to Main Street. Herbie says Hernandez is over at the Mental Court shooting free throws.

"Let's go," I say.

Herbie sits there like he doesn't want to go, but then he stands up. We cross the street and head for the court. "I woulda wore underwear if I knew we were gonna be running around," he says.

As we approach I can see Hernandez hit three in a row. He's got a dark blue Penn State baseball cap on, and long shorts even though it's only about fifty degrees out.

Rico puts both his hands out for the ball, and Hernandez passes it. Rico puts up a long jump shot, which clangs off the metal backboard but doesn't even hit the rim.

"Two-on-two?" Hernandez says.

Herbie says okay. "Let me shoot a few first," he says. He takes the ball and dribbles in, sinking a lay-up. He rebounds it and tosses up a short jumper, which rolls around the rim and out. "Puerto Ricans against whites," he says.

"I'm Cuban," Rico says.

"Whatever. Me and Bones verse you."

None of us is very good, but Hernandez has height and some decent skills. They beat us 10–7. About halfway through I became aware of Shannon and Eileen standing outside the chain-link fence, watching. I acted like I didn't notice.

But as soon as Hernandez puts in the game-winner I stroll over to the fence. I put both arms up and grip the links.

"Hi," I say.

"Hey," they both say.

"What are you up to?" I ask.

"Hanging around," Shannon says.

"Yeah," I say. Herbie's come over now. Rico and Hernandez are playing one-on-one behind us.

"Ladies," Herbie says.

"Herbie," they say.

"Good game," Shannon says.

"Not my best."

"Seen Joey?" Shannon asks.

Herbie looks at me. "I ain't," he says. He clears his throat and spits off to the side. He smiles at Shannon. "What do you need him for when there's men like us around?"

Shannon smiles and shrugs. "He's interesting. And you're sweaty."

Eileen is just standing there this whole time, listening. I guess I am, too. I glance at her. It's been two weeks since the football game, and I never followed up or anything. She's a nice kid, but I'm just not attracted. She's not the one to help me settle my mother's fears.

I look back at Shannon. She squints at me a little, maybe asking a question with her eyes. Asking me why I'm not pursuing Eileen.

Then I say something that surprises me. "Party at my house next Saturday."

Shannon says, "Great."

Herbie says, "My man."

"Don't tell nobody," I say. "This will be real small. Us and a few others."

"Joey?" Shannon says.

"Yeah, of course," I say.

"Cool," says Shannon. "We'll be there."

We steal the steaks on Sunday, but we can only get seven. That will limit the guest list. It's my house, so I'm making the call. I decide on my two fellow midfielders—Hernandez and Rico—plus Herbie, Joey, Shannon, Eileen, and me. I don't really want Eileen there, but I don't have much choice, since I already told her about it. I tell Joey to keep his mouth shut about the party or it'll turn into an open house. No way am I letting that happen.

We get a few other items, and I type up an invitation on our computer:

```
B. David Austin cordially invites you
to an evening of food and fellowship.
         * Saturday, October 22 *
         117 16th St., Sturbridge

  6:30ish: Cocktails
           Celery and olives
           Little cheese crackers
           Chicken wings
  7:15:    Dinner
           Broiled sirloin steak with
              mushroom caps
           Assorted rolls
           Canned peas

* All food courtesy of the Sturbridge Inn *
    Please RSVP by October 19
   (and don't tell nobody else)
```

Joey wants his name on the invitation, too, but this is my house, my risk. So no way. We dub this event the Octoberfest and print seven copies.

I have a real sense of dread about this. I'm not sure why.

We have the steaks stashed in a cooler in Joey's garage. He says he'll change the ice every day. I guess I can count on him for that much.

An Insider's Guide

The dinner hour is slow time in the YMCA
weight room. The after-school and work
people have mostly finished up, and the
evening crowd isn't in yet. You've got a
few paunchy adults on the treadmills and
a solitary guy or two grunting with
forty-pound dumbbells.

The weight room is downstairs, a big open
area with no windows but lots of mirrors.
There's a Universal machine, two inclined
sit-up boards, a bunch of stair-climbers and
cycling machines, and a couple of tons of
weights. The aroma is sweat and powder and
slightly damp carpet.

Three times a week you'll find my brother
Tommy in there, focused on his workout,
steadily doing sets on the bench and racking
up dozens of dips and pull-ups and leglifts.

Sometimes I'm in there with him, doing
about a third as much as he does. I get
distracted, reading the fitness articles
on the bulletin board or sneakily watching
from the corner if there's a nicely built
woman working out.

But the dinner hour is a good time to
be there, if you want to see a champion
in the making.

16
DIRT AND SWEAT

My legs are burning and my chest is pounding from sprinting up and down this field. Time is running out and we're tied 1–1. We need a win badly. Joey's down in the left corner, two guys on him, desperately trying to work his way out. I start moving toward the goal because I've seen Joey get free a thousand times in situations like this.

And suddenly he makes the move, no, a series of moves, turning toward the sideline, touching the ball with his heel and pivoting past one man, then charging by the other. But the second guy recovers, gets a foot on the ball, and it pops up between them. Joey falls back, darting out his right foot as he goes down and lofting the ball in my direction. I get my head on it but not squarely, and the ball bounces over the goal line, out of bounds.

The South goalie sets up for a goal kick. "Nice pass," I say to Joey. It's the type of play that sets him apart from the rest of us, the reason he's so good.

He nods but doesn't look my way, backing up slowly, eyes on the ball. The goalie boots it and one of their midfielders takes it, moving it ahead.

They cross midfield with a couple of crisp passes. Our guys are tired and no one is challenging the ball. The South players work it upfield, then they've got a guy in the clear, slicing toward the goal. Hernandez races in, forcing him toward the goal line. The guy stops the ball and chips it across the goal. Their striker gets a thigh on it, but Joey is there, booting it hard toward the corner, out of bounds.

The ref calls a corner kick and we form a wall. "Let's go!" Joey yells. He's taken the game into his own hands in the past few minutes, playing the whole field, being everywhere. The corner kick is soft and high, floating into the penalty area. We leap, but their striker gets highest, and the ball bullets off his forehead and into the goal.

"Shit!" Joey yells, risking an ejection.

Herbie slaps the goalpost and looks up at the sky.

We can't buy a break lately.

"Line up!" Joey yells, running toward the midfield circle. There might be just enough time for one more penetration, one last try to tie it. Joey takes the kickoff, sliding the ball ahead to Dusty, but Dusty boots it way downfield and a defender easily handles it. Joey sprints across the field toward the ball, but the ref blows the whistle before he can get there.

The South guys leap and embrace each other, running off the field with their fists in the air. I stand there and watch them, then drop to my knees, totally spent. Joey's ten feet away from me with his hands on his hips, staring into space. We stay frozen like that until everybody else is off the field.

Joey turns to me, looking like he can't believe we lost again. "Lazy bunch of assholes," he says.

"Who?"

"Everybody. Everybody but us. We had a chance to win the friggin' league this year, but nobody seems to give a shit. We're losing to teams we should be slaughtering."

We stand there looking at each other. We all want to win,

but it's true that some of us are willing to do more to get it. There's always been a gap between how bad we want it and how bad others do. Even in the peewee leagues, me and Joey always gave every ounce we had in every game.

"Let's go in," he says.

I don't say anything, I just start walking.

We get to the locker room and stand in the doorway. Everybody else is on the benches, and Coach is talking about keeping our heads up. He says we played better today, more aggressive.

"Bullshit," Joey says.

"Excuse me?" Coach says, turning to him.

"I said Bullshit. We got outhustled. Guys were laying back. How the hell can you jog around out there when you got two minutes left in a deadlocked game? I'm tired of playing with people who don't have any guts when it gets tough."

Coach puts out his hand, palm up, like he's yielding the floor to Joey. Joey takes it.

"Some of you guys don't even care if we win." He's staring at Herbie. "You slack off. You smoke, you drink."

"You drink," Rico says.

"Hardly ever," Joey says. "You don't pass because you're jealous. You say shit about me behind my back."

"Whoa," I say. "This ain't about you."

"Like hell it ain't. If you guys wanted to win half as much as I do we'd be undefeated."

I just shake my head. He knows I want it, too.

Joey sits down on the bench and starts untying his shoe.

Everybody's quiet, staring at the floor or into space. Joey's got tears in his eyes, but I think I'm the only one who notices.

Maybe he does want it more than I do. Maybe he scores goals and wins all the wind sprints and gets to make out with Shannon because he won't accept anything less. Maybe I need to face up to that.

The silence breaks with a thud as he flings his shoe into his locker. He gets undressed and walks toward the showers, and the rest of us are still sitting there on the benches in our uniforms.

Coach leaves the room. We sit with our mouths hanging open, eyes fixed on the ceiling or the floor or the lockers. The room smells like dirt and sweat. And the only sound is the hissing of the shower in the other room.

17
LITTLE JUKE

I stop at Joey's house on the way to the school Saturday. We're playing Laurelton at home. We're only 1–2–1 in our last four league games, 5–3–2 overall. We've fallen to third place, but Greenfield has lost another one also, so we can still get back in the race. East Pocono's in first.

We tied Laurelton last month, and they're tough. They upset Greenfield last week. And the way we've been playing we could be in trouble.

Joey's father tells me to come in. He's built like Joey, but a little fat in the face. He says Joey's not ready yet. "The man worked until midnight last night," he says.

"At the restaurant?"

"Yeah. Somebody called in sick, so he went in. He said it was packed."

"It usually is on Fridays."

I look around the living room, which is loaded with trophies and plaques. Lots of them are Joey's, but not all. There's Sturbridge Little League Coach of the Year. Fifth Place, Masters Division, Greater Scranton Triathlon. Champion, Men's Kayak, Pocono Whitewater Classic.

"Big game today," he says. "You guys need a win."

"We sure do," I say.

"Just get the ball to the man," he says, winking at me. "Get the ball to the man."

⊛　⊛　⊛

The team is quiet warming up, but we seem more focused. We've got a lot to prove to ourselves. I haven't heard one word from anybody about Joey's tirade after the last game, but I know it's on everybody's mind.

We've got four games left: Laurelton today and Midvale on Wednesday, then East Pocono and Greenfield the following week. We lose any one of them and we're finished. Even a tie might put us out of the race.

Joey is over on the sidelines with a ball, juggling and stretching. He hardly said anything on the way here. I tried a couple of times to get a conversation going, but he just mumbled and shrugged. The rest of us are shooting at Herbie, going two-on-one.

It's a sunny day, warm and breezy. We probably have the biggest crowd in Sturbridge soccer history, about two hundred people. Joey's parents are here. Shannon and Eileen, too. Even Herbie's parents.

Coach calls us over. "New beginning," he says. "Look inside yourselves, fellas. You can start fresh today or you can pack it in. It's up to you."

We're all quiet for a few seconds. "Anything to say?" Coach asks. "Joey?"

Joey shakes his head.

"Dusty?"

"Just kick ass."

"Anybody else?"

More quiet. Coach says, "Let's go," and we trot onto the field.

⊗   ⊗   ⊗

Joey scores about three minutes into the game, taking a pass from Trunk, maintaining control of the ball as he fights through a pack of defenders, and driving it deep into the net. The crowd yells like crazy, but nobody on the field says much.

Joey scores again midway through the second quarter, receiving a throw-in from Hernandez, sprinting toward the goal line, stopping short and pivoting as a defender overruns him, and bulleting it into the goal from twenty feet out.

He makes it 3–0 just after halftime, intercepting a pass at midfield, going straight down the center, turning his back on a midfielder, then knocking the ball between the guy's legs, recovering the ball, and simply outrunning that midfielder and a defender, heading straight toward the right corner of the goal but managing to drive the ball in the opposite direction, sending it cleanly into the upper left.

The crowd goes wild. Joey keeps a stern expression on his face, not looking at any of us.

Coach brings in some subs for the fourth quarter and puts me and Rico on the front line with Joey and Trunk. It's my first chance to play forward this season.

Late in the game Joey nearly scores again, sending a high, hard shot toward the upper right corner of the goal. Their goalie leaps and gets a hand on it, deflecting it over the crossbar.

We set up for a corner kick; Trunk's taking it. He lofts it in front of the goal, and everybody goes up for a header. One of their guys gets it, but he doesn't hit it far and I get control near the top of the box. I take one step toward the goal, then slide it to my left, where Rico is open. He knocks it forward and gives a quick fake to his right. The goalie takes the fake, dodging in that same direction, and Rico kicks it past him into the goal.

Rico throws both fists into the air and I run over and grab him around the waist, lifting him off the ground. We sprint back toward midfield, and Hernandez comes running up to meet us. It's Rico's first goal for this team.

We're back in a groove now, playing like champions. When the game ends Herbie takes his shirt off and twirls it around his head. We're yelling and clapping and jumping up and down. Rico goes around slapping palms with everybody.

Everybody but Joey, who walked off the field alone.

Rico's still flying, so psyched about scoring. He's sitting on the bench in just his shorts, reliving the moment. Herbie's on the floor with a can of Coke, leaning against his locker.

"See, I gave him that little juke and he went for it," Rico's saying. "He left the whole side of the goal open for me."

"He got suckered," Herbie says.

"That's what makes you so effective," Rico says. "You never go for that first fake, Herbie."

I look over at Joey, standing by the door, already dressed to leave. I'm getting ready to give up on this guy if he's going to keep being such a prick. He's staring at us. I catch his eye.

"Don't get carried away," he says.

Rico frowns at him. "Get bent," he says.

"It was one win," Joey says. "We got a long way to go before we've got a reason to celebrate."

"Oh, take a hike, Joey," Herbie says. "You made your point last time. None of us is as committed as you are, none of us has any guts."

"It's true," Joey says.

"Get a life."

"Got one."

"Do you?"

"Better than yours."

"Is it?"

Joey shakes his head. He calls Herbie a dirtbag.

Herbie gives Joey a salute and says, "Yes, sir, General."

Joey salutes back, but with just one finger. Then he pushes open the door and leaves the room.

Herbie turns to Rico. "What a jackass," he says. And they both crack up. I laugh, too, but not as hard as they do.

18
THE OCTOBERFEST

The guests are fashionably late in arriving, but by 6:50 all seven of us are present. I've got the gas grill going on the patio and we're sitting at the kitchen table munching olives and chicken wings and drinking lemonade spiked with vodka.

Joey keeps saying how tired he is, reminding us that he worked late last night and ran his ass off in the game today. Plus he has to be in by midnight because his parents are concerned about a bad grade in algebra.

I get up and take the plate of steaks out of the refrigerator. I had them marinating in soy sauce and parsley. "How does everybody want these?" I ask.

Everybody says medium except Herbie, who wants his extra well done.

"You might as well eat dirt," Joey says with a sneer.

"You might as well eat shit," Herbie answers.

Joey glares at him. Shannon pats Joey's hand. "What difference does it make how he eats it?" she says.

"No difference," Joey says. "It's just stupid to cremate a nice piece of meat."

Shannon laughs. She makes a fist and shows it to Herbie. "He'll kick your ass if you ruin that steak," she says. "And I'll help him."

Herbie puts up both palms. "Whoa. I'm shaking."

She gets up and puts Herbie in a headlock, rubbing her

fist gently into his jaw. "You bastard," she says. "Charring that poor little steak."

Herbie's faking like he's in agony. Joey shoves back from the table and stands up. He goes out into the living room and turns the TV on to the Penn State football game. He doesn't come back until I say the steaks are ready.

When I come in with the meat everybody else is at the table and the only empty seat is next to Eileen. Shannon's sitting between Rico and Herbie.

The girls only want half a steak apiece, so Hernandez takes Shannon's other half and Herbie says he'll take Eileen's. He reaches over and stabs it with his fork, then gets up to put it back on the grill.

"There he goes again with the incineration," Joey says, sounding disgusted.

Herbie just grins. "What the hell do you care?"

"Just sit down and eat the thing like a man," Joey says.

Herbie shakes his head. "Okay, Dad," he says. But he goes out to the patio anyway.

Shannon gets up and says she's going to floss her teeth. Joey finishes his steak and goes back out to the TV.

Other than that things go pretty smoothly until about quarter to nine, when the bell rings. I open the door and there's Tony Terranova with four of his friends and a couple of cases of beer.

"Bones, my man," he says.

"Tony."

"Thought we'd keep you company."

"You did, huh?" This could be trouble, but Tony's not a bad guy. Plus he has a few items with him that would help the party: the beer and the friends, since two of them are girls. "Why not?" I say, and I step aside to let them in.

They station themselves at the kitchen table and put the beer in the refrigerator. I sit out there, too, and we talk about music and stuff, concerts we've been to in Scranton.

The two girls are cute. Dana and Staci. They're both juniors. Dana has long brown hair. Staci is black, with her hair gathered in a ponytail and one tiny gold earring. The guys are all wrestlers.

Eileen comes into the kitchen after a while and asks me if there's any lemonade left. I say I don't know, but I get up to check. There's enough for half a glass, so I pour it for her.

"Thanks," she says. "You're missing some fun out there."

"I'm having fun in here," I say.

"Everybody's dancing," she says.

I nod. "Not me."

"Oh," she says. She looks into the glass, then takes a sip. She shrugs her shoulders and heads back into the living room.

Staci looks at Dana and they both shake their heads. "Oooh, ooh, Bones," Staci says. "She's aching for you."

"No, thanks," I say.

"She's not so bad," Dana says.

I just roll my eyes.

"Go dance with her," Staci says.

"I don't think so."

Staci clicks her tongue. "Don't be a hard boy."

"Not interested."

"You're no fun."

I lock eyes with her and smile. "I could be."

She smiles back but shakes her head slowly. "I think I'll go out and dance," she says. She winks at me. "Come on, Dana," she says.

By ten o'clock Tony and the two guys he brought with him are pretty drunk, and they're getting loud. When the phone rings I yell, "Everybody shut up! Turn off the stereo."

I pick up the phone. It's my mother.

"Everything okay, Barry?" she asks.

"Yeah."

"What are you up to?"

"Nothing much. Joey came over. That's okay, right?"

"Sure. How did you do today?"

"Good. We shut them out. We seem to be back on track."

"I'm glad."

"Um, is Tommy there with you?" I ask.

"Yes. Just a sec."

I hear her say his name. After a few seconds he takes the phone.

"What's up?" he asks.

"I got a situation here."

"Yeah?"

"Terranova and some of your other friends showed up."

"And?"

"I wanna get rid of them."

"Oh."

"I know you can't talk," I say.

"Right."

"I was having some people over. Not too many. They must have heard about it."

"Hmmm . . ." he says. "So we'll try to go fishing next weekend, maybe."

"What?"

"We'll talk about it later." He kind of emphasizes "later."

Five minutes later the phone rings again. I yell, "Shut up and turn off the stereo" again.

"Hello?" I say.

"It's me." Tommy.

"Yeah."

"I'm in my own room now. What's going on?"

"Nothing bad. Just more people than I wanted."

"Let me talk to Tony."

I call Tony over and he takes the phone. "It's my brother," I tell him.

"Yo," Tony says. "Yeah. . . . No. . . . No. . . . We're not. . . . Dana. . . . Her, too. . . . Yeah. . . . Sure. . . . Right." He hands the phone back to me.

"What?" I say to Tommy.

"They'll be gone by eleven."

"Okay."

"They'll take all the beer cans with them, too."

"Good."

"Listen," he says. "Tomorrow morning, or even tonight after everybody leaves, check under the furniture for empty cans or used glasses. And check the wastebaskets in the bathrooms. Tomorrow check the yard. I got nailed once because somebody left an empty Jack Daniel's pint under the couch."

"When was that?"

"Last year. You guys went to Aunt Beth's for the weekend for Katie's christening. I had too much studying to do."

"Right."

"Shannon there?"

"Yeah."

"Uh-huh." I can almost hear him smile.

"Joey's here, too," I say.

"Too bad. See you tomorrow."

"Okay, man. Thanks."

I stay in the kitchen for a while, avoiding the living room, where Eileen is. When I stick my head out there I notice that Joey is asleep in the armchair. I catch Herbie's eye and he grins, nodding his head slowly. He walks over to the kitchen. Rico comes, too.

"He's gotta be home at twelve, right?" Herbie asks.

"Yeah."

"Let's help him along," he says, reaching for the clock above the sink. He takes it down and moves the hands ahead an hour and a half to 12:15. Then he asks, "Where else?"

"There's one on the mantel in the living room," I say.

He goes out and resets that one, a digital clock radio.

Rico says, "He got a watch on?"

We look, but he doesn't.

Everybody else is dancing or drinking and seems oblivious to what we're doing. But Shannon steps over to me and asks what's going on.

"Nothing," I say. "A little joke."

She smirks. "Poor Joey," she says.

"You wanna wake him up?"

"Ummm, no," she says. "I don't want to be a part of this."

"I'll do it," Herbie says. He walks over to the CD player and turns the volume up full, just for a second. Joey opens his eyes. We try to act like we haven't even noticed him sleeping.

Joey rubs his eyes and stands up. He walks across the room to the bathroom. When he comes out he glances at the clock on the mantel and says, "Shit." The clock shows 12:22.

"I'm screwed," he says. He looks around for his jacket, finding it in a pile on the couch. "I'm outta here," he says, bolting out the door.

Herbie pumps his fist and yells "Yes!" after the door slams shut. He slaps hands with Rico. Shannon shakes her head but laughs.

"What's going on?" Eileen asks.

"Sleeping Beauty just turned into a pumpkin," Herbie says, mixing up his literary references.

Eileen looks at the clock. "Oh, you guys are cruel," she says, but she's laughing, too. It's a harmless joke.

Terranova taps me on the shoulder. "We're going," he says. He's got a full six-pack and another with two cans missing under his arm. "Thanks, Bones." And the five of them leave, too.

That leaves six of us. I set the clocks back to 11:03. Hernandez is dancing with Shannon, but that doesn't mean anything. Rico starts dancing with Eileen. Me and Herbie just watch for a few minutes, then go out in the kitchen to eat the rest of the chicken wings.

Shannon comes in after a while and sits at the table. She's wearing a denim shirt, with the top two buttons undone.

"Herbie, could you guys get Eileen home safely?" she says. "I need to talk to Bones."

About Joey, I figure. Herbie says, "Sure. Now?"

"In a while," she says. "Whenever." She goes back into the living room. I can hear them laughing out there.

Herbie's picking chicken out of his teeth with a fingernail. "Brace yourself," he says.

"What for?"

"Whatever," he says. "She's up to something."

When they leave I start washing the dishes, and Shannon gets a towel to dry them. Our arms keep bumping.

"Great party," she says.

"Yeah," I say. "It went all right."

"Those guys are a riot," she says.

"True."

"Don't you dance?" she asks.

"Not often," I say. "Hardly ever."

She puts one hand on my shoulder and looks at my face. "Joey just sat there all night," she says.

"He was tired," I say.

"He was nasty."

"He's under a lot of pressure," I say.

"From who?"

"His father. Himself. Us."

"Yeah, well, that's tough," she says. "I was dancing with Herbie, and Joey was staring at us like he wanted to kill us both."

"He's worried about you."

"That's ridiculous," she says. "He knows Herbie cracks me up. It's nothing."

"I guess it isn't to him."

She runs her hand down my arm and squeezes my wrist. "That was great how you guys got rid of him," she says. "I had a much better time after he left." She runs her hand back up my arm and across my shoulders. "You didn't seem to mind a whole lot when Eileen left, either."

I chew on my lip and scrub the plate I'm washing a little harder than I need to. "Eileen's okay," I finally say. "She's just not, you know, not right for me."

Shannon turns her back to the sink and leans against the counter. "Yeah," she says, inching closer to me. She knocks her knee gently against my leg. "Well, you know," she whispers, "I don't taste like puke."

And she doesn't. She tastes minty and lemony. And God, she feels nice. She's lean and solid. And warm. We work our way to the couch.

We lie there, pressed tight against each other, making out nonstop for at least an hour. It's exhausting.

I walk her home about one o'clock, avoiding Main Street. Not many people are out. She lives up past the school, so we walk along Maple. I've got my arm around her waist and she's got her hand in my back pocket.

This feels more than a little strange, like I've taken a candy bar from Rite Aid without paying, or as if a referee didn't see me knock the ball out of bounds and awarded me a throw-in.

Her house is halfway up Buchanan Street, which is steep and dark. We stop on her walk.

She puts her hands on my shoulders. Her smile is . . . I

don't know, ironic or something. I lean forward and kiss her, and she lets me linger there a few seconds. I don't know if this is the beginning of something or the end. She turns toward the door. "See ya," she says.

"Okay." I stand there with my hands in my pockets until she's closed the door and turned off the outside light. I feel warm, and mostly satisfied. Mostly happy.

I walk down the street toward the school, scuffing through some piles of leaves. The air is cool and still, and sort of misty. I cross the street and go into the stadium, hurrying down the cement bleachers and onto the track.

I'm feeling detached, like my world is spinning just a little too fast and I've lost the connection between my imagination and my body. Maybe that's because, for once, my body has eclipsed my imagination, actually doing something that I've previously only wondered about.

I start to jog, feeling the pat-pat-pat of my feet against the track. I'm probably a better runner than I am a soccer player. I run the 400 and 800 in the spring, but that's a different side of me. The side that's more like Tommy.

I reach the backstretch and move a little faster, my arms swinging smoothly and my breathing feeling right. After a couple of laps I'm sweating, so I toss my jacket into an outside lane and pull my shirt out of my pants. I can taste my own sweat now, mixing with Shannon on my lips.

I'm driving hard, in a higher gear, not hurting at all. I asked Tommy once why he runs cross-country, why he keeps at it when he isn't very good. And he said he wouldn't care if he was the slowest guy in Pennsylvania, because every step he takes makes him a tiny fraction tougher, gets him closer to the state championship in wrestling.

After another mile I start sprinting, really letting go. I'll sprint for as long as I can take it, until I can't do another step. I'm into the turn now, the white painted lines forming a pathway. Down the homestretch, the acid building in my legs, my arms beginning to tighten. I take it even harder on the far turn and power into the backstretch.

My chest is heaving as I begin to slow, my jaw is tense. I ease into a jog, lifting my arms above my head and sucking in air. When I reach my jacket I pick it up, dragging it behind me as I slow to a walk.

Lots of people jog on this track, but not very many ever sprint here late at night. I like that idea. I like to be places where no one ever goes, or go places at times when no one else ever would. So being here, now, feels all mine.

It must be nearly two as I walk back along Maple. I look up Buchanan Street; Shannon's house is dark. I can see Main Street below me; it's quiet and empty.

I have lots to think about tomorrow. But I'll sleep good tonight.

19
WORK

Of course I have to face Joey Sunday night. He's already in when I get there, standing over by the dishwasher.

"How's it going?" I say, putting too much enthusiasm in my voice.

He looks at me without smiling. "Yeah," he says, turning away.

I feel the ice. He knows. I don't know how, but he knows.

I try again. "Watch the Giants this afternoon?" He always watches the Giants games with his father.

"Nope," he says. There are no dishes yet, but he takes one of the dish trays off the stack and sets it on the counter.

"Guess I better punch in," I say. I go into the office and punch my time card, then go in the back to wait for something to do.

Maybe he's just pissed off about the clock thing, but I doubt he even figured that out. And he couldn't have seen anything coming between me and Shannon, because even I didn't read that one.

I have not told a single soul, and I can't imagine that she'd tell him. And she wouldn't tell Eileen, either. Neither of us would have anything to gain, and we'd probably lose our best friends over this. Maybe we already have.

About 8:30 I slip into the office and dial Shannon's number. She's real friendly when I tell her it's me.

"You home?" she asks.

"No. I'm at work."

"Oh," she says. "Ohhh," she repeats, as it dawns on her that I'm with Joey.

"You talk to him today?" I ask.

"No."

"Oh."

"Why?"

"I don't know," I say. "He seems pissed."

"Oh. You think he knows?"

"I don't know. How could anybody know?"

"I don't know."

We're both quiet for a few seconds. Then she says, "I didn't tell anybody."

"Yeah. I didn't, either. He's been a jerk lately. He's just pissed in general, I guess."

"Probably," she says. "It's no big deal anyway. Listen, I gotta go."

"Oh. Okay. See ya."

"Okay."

"Wait," I say.

"What?"

"It was no big deal?" I'm trying not to sound hurt.

"Not really. Was it?"

"Um, I guess not."

"It was nice." She sounds consoling.

"Yeah."

"You're sweet, Bones. We'll talk about it sometime."

"Okay."

I hang up. Shit. Kenny's standing in the doorway. "You ain't supposed to use that phone," he says.

"It was an emergency."

"I bet."

I stand up and stare him down. "I was on for like twenty seconds."

"Tell it to Carlos."

I just shake my head and walk past him into the kitchen. I guess he's a big authority figure now or something. And like he never uses the phone, right?

There's only been about eight customers all night, so I could just sit in the back and eat carrots if I wanted. But I figure I'm getting paid to be here, so I ought to help Joey with the cleanup. I walk over by the dishwasher and wait for a tray to come out. When it does, I go to grab it, but Joey reaches it first. "I got this stuff," he says, not looking at me. "Do the pots."

I shrug and walk away.

I go out by the Dumpster and look at the sky. It's a clear night, kind of cool.

This is awkward, having the upper hand on Joey for once. I've been his sidekick for a long time, the quiet guy behind the scenes. And even though he's still the bigger sports star, I've moved a step ahead of him in certain ways. I've got a wider circle of friends, that's for sure. Without me, in fact, I don't think he has any.

And when you come down to it, I think he's more upset about my hanging out with Herbie and Rico than he'd be if he knew about Shannon.

But I can't say I feel good about all this.

I stare at the sky for five more minutes. Then I go in to take care of the pots.

What does she mean, it was no big deal?

⊗   ⊗   ⊗

Monday before practice Coach sits us down in the locker room
and gives us the lowdown on our chances to win the league.

"We got three games left and we need to win them all,"
he says. "Plus we need some help."

We've got Midvale on Wednesday, then we close with
East Pocono and Greenfield, the two teams ahead of us.

"If you think you can look past Midvale, think again,"
Coach says. "They beat Greenfield on Saturday. Anything
can happen in this league, including us winning it all. But
you'd better be prepared to run your asses into the ground
for the next week and a half."

He points to the blackboard, where he's got the standings
written. East Pocono is in first at 7–2–2, and they still have
to play Greenfield, us, and Midvale.

Greenfield's next at 7–3–1, with East Pocono, Mount
Ridge, and us still to play.

We're third at 6–3–2.

I catch Rico's eye. He squints and nods. Everybody looks
determined, even Herbie, who doesn't usually pay atten-
tion during meetings.

I go out about nine Monday night, walking up to Main
Street. Herbie and Rico are on the bench, but I hesitate,
then go into Turkey Hill. I was hoping Herbie might be out
alone. I need somebody to talk to.

I look at the magazines, then buy a large bag of potato
chips and go out to the bench.

"Didn't expect to see you tonight," Herbie says, taking a
handful of potato chips.

"I was restless," I say. "Anybody else been out?"

"Trunk was. And your friend Joey."

"He was?"

"Yeah. He asked if we'd seen you."

"What'd you say?"

They look at each other and laugh. "We told him you were probably with his girlfriend," Herbie says.

"You *did*?"

"Yeah."

"Man, you guys suck." I fold my arms and shake my head. "What did he say?"

"He just sneered and threatened to beat me up, like he always does," Herbie says. "Then he walked away. Like he always does."

"Herbie, how do you know everything that happens whenever I'm with a girl?"

"I'm well connected," he says.

"Nobody saw us."

He gives me this tilted-head, raised-eyebrows look that indicates that somebody did.

"Who?" I say.

"Nobody. But you just confirmed what everybody was thinking."

"It doesn't matter," I say.

"No?"

I shake my head. "It'll never happen again."

"Why not?"

"I don't know. It was just one of those things."

"Hope you made the most of it," he says.

I don't know how to answer that one. I take another

handful of potato chips, then hand the bag to Rico. I crumble the chips in my hand and let the crumbs fall to the sidewalk. Then I wipe my hand on my jacket and stand up. "Thanks a lot, guys," I say.

"Anytime," Herbie answers.

An Insider's Guide

Before you reach the top of the cliff
overlooking the town, there's a path you
can turn onto to work your way downhill
through the woods. Eventually you come to
a clearing with twelve apple trees planted
in three rows of four about fifteen yards
apart. The trees are old and uncared for,
but they get heavy with fruit in the fall,
and deer hang out there.

The second tree in the second row has two
parallel limbs about seven feet off the
ground, just thick enough to grip with your
fists, but strong enough to support your
weight.

With the first few pull-ups the branches
spring lightly, and a bit of the tree's
resilience seems to pass into your forearms
and shoulders. But as the effort increases,
as your own limbs begin to burn and the pace
begins to slow, it becomes a struggle
against the tree. The tree always wins. But
sometimes you last just a little bit longer.

It's a good place to go when you're angry
or frustrated or have more energy than you
know what to do with.

Not even my brother knows that I come
here. But he's probably the only one in
Sturbridge who would understand.

20
MOVING FORWARD

When I got to work Tuesday night there was this guy Larry from day shift running the dishwasher. I asked Kenny where Joey was, and he said he called in sick, which is bullshit. He wasn't sick at practice. He was a grouch, but he hustled as much as ever.

So I spent the night in the back doing pots and listening to the country music station on the radio, which is the only station Kenny lets us play. Larry is older, in his twenties, and doesn't say much. He takes the job seriously, even though he obviously hates every second of it. So I didn't say a word the whole night.

If Joey's angry enough to not even be able to work with me, I don't see how we're going to function on the soccer field. But we've got Midvale tomorrow, and every game is crucial the rest of the way.

I'll just pretend he's somebody else when I have to pass him the ball.

Halfway through the second quarter I take a pass near the top corner of their penalty area. Midvale is playing a conservative game, getting everybody back on defense, so it's been tough to find anybody open.

I see Joey running toward the goal, but there's a Midvale player between me and him. I can't get the ball to Joey, but I see where he's going. So I pass into the space beyond the defender, who turns and gets into a race with Joey for the ball. Joey gets there first, wins control, and fires the ball into the goal.

He puts his fist in the air as he runs back toward midfield. Trunk and Dusty give him high fives. I catch his eye, but he just looks away.

We go up 2–0 before the half when Trunk heads one in off a corner kick.

Joey gets a good opportunity to score again in the third quarter, taking control of a deflected shot in the goal box. Two steps gets him to point-blank range, and the goalie desperately lunges toward that side of the goal. Joey stops short, dodges right, and crosses the ball in front of the goal. I'm coming straight in, anticipating a rebound, but all I have to do is field the ball and walk it into the net. Great pass. Smart move.

I slap hands with Trunk and sprint back toward the center circle. Joey's running parallel to me, but he won't look my way. We're up 3–0.

We won't talk to each other, but at least we're playing like a team.

Joey made it 4–0 before Coach started substituting heavily. So we've got two straight shutouts and a 7–3–2 record. Coach comes in the locker room after the game and tells us that Greenfield beat East Pocono to move into first. So we're tied with East Pocono for second in the league, and we play them on Monday.

Trunk stands up on the wooden bench in front of his locker and yells, "We're number one! We . . . will . . . kick . . . their . . . BUTTS!"

Guys start yelling and pounding on the lockers. Herbie climbs onto the bench next to Trunk and raises both arms. He's naked, and with his arms outstretched like that you can see his ribs. "Nothing gets through me, my friends," he says. "This body is unbeatable. These hands"—he turns his palms outward and spreads the fingers—"will let no ball get by!"

We let up a cheer. Herbie's got his eyes shut and his fingers extended toward the ceiling. Then he leaps off the bench and lands in the center of the room.

Trunk starts pounding his fist rhythmically against his locker. Guys start clapping in time and stamping their feet. We feel like a team for the first time in ages. I look around at these guys—Rico's eyes are sparkling with confidence; Hernandez has a big grin and a look of desire; even Dusty looks like he's stopped hating all of us.

This is great. Joey's not here to enjoy it, of course. He grabbed his stuff and ducked right out without even changing clothes. But I won't let that pull me down. I'm moving forward. I'm part of a team.

This season is far from over.

21
PAYBACK

"You going to pick up your check?" I ask Joey after practice on Thursday.

"Got it at lunchtime," he says, staring straight ahead into his locker.

I just shrug. Screw him. I take off all my stuff and towel dry. I'll shower at home. I get dressed and head for the door.

I walk the eight blocks up to the restaurant by myself and go in the back way. Kenny's at the sink cleaning some lettuce. He looks up at me and nods as I walk toward Carlos's office.

I stick my head in the office. Carlos is at his desk, talking on the phone. He raises one finger, telling me to wait. In a minute he sets down the phone and swivels his chair toward me.

"Hi," I say. "Just wanted my check."

"Your check," he repeats.

"Yeah."

He starts tapping the desk with one finger. "Why don't you come in and sit down?" he says.

So I do.

He raises his eyebrows and looks at me hard for a few seconds. "How are you, Bones?"

"Good. . . . I'm okay."

"That's good." He hands me an envelope. It's not my paycheck. "Do you recognize this?" he asks.

I take out a folded paper and feel a cold sweat breaking out. It's an Octoberfest invitation.

"An interesting document," he says.

I bite down on my lip and look around.

"Is that your work?" Carlos asks.

"Uh . . . yeah."

"I think you know better than that," he says.

I rub my chin, not sure what to do. "I'll pay for the stuff," I finally say.

He smiles, but it's not a happy smile. "Your take-home pay this week would have been about forty dollars," he says. "Suppose we call it even?"

That sounds like a good deal to me. "Seems fair," I say.

"Oh, it's more than fair," he says. "You're lucky that I like you, son. You've been a good worker."

"Thanks."

"But you can't work here any longer."

"Shit," I whisper, but I'm getting off easy. "I'm sorry."

He nods. "I don't want to see you here again," he says.

"Okay." I let out a sigh and blink hard.

Kenny is in the doorway. "Trouble?" he asks Carlos.

"A bit," Carlos says. "It's under control, thank you."

Kenny's got his arms folded. He shifts his weight from one foot to the other. "You ask him about the silverware?" Kenny asks.

"Kenny, I'm handling this," he says. "Please get back to work."

Kenny glares at me and backs away. It's pretty clear that he had something to do with this. But that menu could only have gotten to Carlos from one source. And I think I know where to find him.

I stand up to leave. "See ya," I say.

"Good-bye."

Kenny's back at the sink as I walk past. "Your buddy says you spit in the mayonnaise," he says.

"I don't have any buddies working here," I say, heading out the door.

It takes about thirty seconds to reach Herbie's bench. Rico's there, too. "Where's Joey?"

"The Mental Court," Rico answers.

I head off in that direction, and they get up from the bench and follow. I'm walking fast. It's only a block and a half to the court, and my heart is beating a mile a minute.

"Hey, Joey!" I holler. "Get over here!"

He's down at the far end of the court in a three-on-three game, but he comes right over. He had to be expecting this.

He comes up to me and walks right into my first punch, which catches him just below the eye.

He backs away and wipes his cheek, but he doesn't ask what this is about. He comes right at me, grabbing my shirt and swinging. But I'm too close; the punch just glances off my shoulder. He curses and tries to tackle me, but I bob away and call him an asshole.

It turns into a wrestling match, trying to throw each other down. He gets the advantage and knocks me backward, but I get my balance, feint left, and swing hard and miss.

Then he lands a good one; knuckles against the side of my head. There's a split-second flash, like a bright light I don't see but sense. Or maybe I see it, but not with my eyes;

I see it with the back of my brain. And I'm down on all fours, but I hop right back up. One shake and my head's clear, clear enough to keep going, to swing with everything I've got and miss. But I come back with another, not as potent but this time connecting, and Joey is bleeding from the mouth.

There's about ten guys watching and yelling, but it's an adult who pulls us apart. He says something about getting the cops, but it sounds like he probably doesn't want to. Before I know what's going on I'm a block away from the basketball court, sitting on the steps of the Episcopal church. Herbie and Rico and a few others are standing there. I feel a lump above my temple and my lip is stinging, but everything else seems intact.

"I win?" I say, to nobody in particular.

22
THE TRUTH

Joey's sitting on the bench in front of his locker talking to Trunk when I get to practice Friday. He looks at me but doesn't say anything. There's a bruise the size of a quarter on his cheek.

My lip is a little puffy, but I manage a tiny smirk. I turn my back on him and open my locker.

Other guys start coming in now. I take off my clothes and start taping my ankles. Joey and Trunk and some others go out to the field.

Herbie comes in and says, "Hey, Bones. When's the rematch?"

"Which one?" I say.

"You and your best friend. You didn't finish."

"Didn't we?"

"No way. We have to resolve this thing, get it out of the way. It pains me to see this rift between you guys, this cleavage."

I shake my head. It must have taken him hours to think up that one. I notice Coach standing in the doorway, but Herbie hasn't seen him.

"Come on, Bones," Herbie says. "Winner gets to make believe he's still got a chance with Shannon."

That hurts a bit, but I laugh.

"Herbie," Coach says.

Herbie gives an *oh, shit* look and turns to Coach.

Coach raises his eyebrows. He teaches seventh grade, so he has a pretty high tolerance for guys acting like jackasses.

"Just giving my man here a pep talk," Herbie says.

"So I see," Coach says. He gives a half-smile that's close to a frown.

Herbie turns to me. "So let's get out there and really work today," he says, holding up a fist. "I'll be outside, doing push-ups." He leaves in a hurry.

Coach comes over to me. "You all right?" he says.

"Sure."

"Get it out of your system?"

"Probably."

"You guys have to stay focused," he says.

"We will."

"Channel that anger into the game."

I nod. I finish getting my soccer stuff on, then go out to the field for practice.

Saturday afternoon I go with my parents over to Scranton to watch the league cross-country championships. I sit in the back of the car and we listen to an old Harry Chapin tape of my father's.

Every few minutes my mother turns to me and asks me something, trying to keep up a conversation. She asks about Joey—she doesn't know about the fight—but I only give one-word answers.

She asks me how the team is; says it's nice that I'm in a group with a common goal to strive for. I say yeah, it is.

She asks whether I'm thinking about going to the prom, and I remind her that I'm only a sophomore. Then she gives up asking me anything. I feel for her. She's just worried about me. But I don't feel like sharing information these days.

We get to the park. The girls' JV race is already under way, so Tommy will be running soon. We walk over near the starting line, and I see him jogging off to the side with a few of his teammates.

When his race starts my parents start shouting, "Come on, Tommy! Get up there!"

I jog a couple hundred yards to a spot where I can see the runners when they double back at the midpoint. I head to the top of a little hill and can see most of the race from there.

Laurelton's varsity is a powerhouse, so their leftover guys are dominating the JV race. They've got the first two places when they run past me, and two others in the top ten. But Tommy's running a great race; he's in twelfth place, second guy for Sturbridge.

"Looking good," I say as he goes by. There's a big pack right on his tail, but he looks strong. I watch a few more people run by, then jog back across to the finish area.

There's a long grassy straightaway that leads to the finish, and spectators are lined up on both sides. I look across that straightaway and suddenly I see Shannon, looking across at me. She waves with a big smile.

I didn't expect to see her here. This might be good. The leaders are approaching, so I can't cut over to her now. But there are two varsity races still to come, so I'll get a chance to hang with her for a while. I wonder how she got here.

The two Laurelton guys come sprinting in together, way ahead of everybody else. Then there's a rush of five or six runners, one after the other. And then here comes Tommy, running the best race of his life. I start clapping. "Way to go!" I holler.

I walk down to the finish chute and meet him at the end. "Great job," I say, putting out my hand.

"Thanks," he says. "Felt good."

I hear Shannon's voice. "Nice race, Tommy," she says.

"Hi," I say, looking up at her. And suddenly I know how she got here because Tony Terranova is there, too.

"Hey, Tony," I say.

"Hey, Bones," he says. They aren't touching or anything, but this doesn't look good. Not that I have any real expectations about me and her anymore. But I hadn't given up entirely.

Tony's got a car. He's a senior. He's got a big-time attitude. I guess her being with him doesn't surprise me. But I think he'd lose interest if he knew about me and her.

This is the first Sunday night I've had free in a while. It's cold and rainy, but I can't stand staring out my window and I don't feel like being downstairs. I told my parents on the way back from Scranton yesterday that I'd been laid off, which isn't entirely a lie.

I've spent most of the day in my room. Actually I've been in here for about twenty-four hours, except to shower and eat. I'm bored and down. And I hate to admit it, but I'm lonely.

About seven o'clock I put on a hooded sweatshirt and a windbreaker and go downstairs. My mother's in the living room. I tell her I need to get something at Turkey Hill.

"It's a miserable night," she says.

"I don't care," I answer.

I walk up to Main. The rain isn't too bad, but nobody's out. Not even Herbie.

A big gust of wind sends a cardboard pumpkin decoration past me and across Main Street. Tomorrow is Halloween. It's also the day we play East Pocono. The loser is eliminated from the race for the championship. If we win it'll set up a showdown with Greenfield.

I get to Turkey Hill and go in, but I don't really want anything. I get a pack of Oreos and a can of Coke, then walk a half block up to the movie theater. The entrance is all boarded up, but there's enough of a ledge that I can sit in the doorway just clear of the rain.

I sit there for half an hour, finishing the Oreos but not even opening the Coke. Maybe six cars go by the whole time.

Eventually I look up Main Street, toward the light, and I see somebody walking in this direction in a yellow windbreaker with the hood up. When he gets to me he sits down. He nods but doesn't say anything.

We stare out at the rain, which is a little steadier now. "Coke?" I say, holding up the can.

"No, thanks," Tommy says.

I let out my breath and it swirls away in a mist. A blue pickup truck goes slowly past on the other side with one headlight burned out. I pull at a loose thread on my jeans. "So what's up with Tony?" I say.

He shrugs. "They went to the movies last night," he says.

"Oh."

"You might not be ready for somebody like her yet," he says softly. Normally a comment like that would piss me off, but he isn't busting my chops. He's telling the truth.

"There's other girls," he says.

"I know." I start drumming lightly with two fingers on the top of the Coke can. "I know."

"Hey," he says, brightening a bit. "At least you're trying."

I give a half-smile. Tommy's had girlfriends on and off since sixth grade, although it's been a while since he had one. That doesn't seem to bother him.

He must sense what I'm thinking. "You can't measure yourself by who you go out with," he says. "Or what they look like."

I nod. But he knows as well as I do how hard it is not to measure yourself that way. You size yourself up against everybody else by the girls you've been with, by the games you've won, by the guys who hang out in your group. They prop up your image; it's hard to stand up on your own.

We're quiet for about five more minutes. A few cars go by and the wind gusts again. Tommy stretches out his arms and yawns. "You and Joey work things out?" he asks.

"Not yet," I say.

He nods slowly. "You will."

"I know it," I say, just above a whisper. "I know it."

23
HALLOWEEN

The wind has blown the field dry by game time, and it's turned colder. There are light snow flurries and the sky is slate gray.

Nobody has to say anything about how important this one is. We're quiet and intense warming up.

Coach calls me over. "Where's your head today?" he asks.

"Right here."

"You sure?"

"Absolutely."

He puts his hand on my shoulder. "Hey, Joey!" he yells.

Joey's down near the goal stretching. "Yeah?" he yells back.

"Come here."

Joey jogs over. He's looking at the bleachers. There are a lot of people here, but he's got his eyes fixed on the same place I had mine: Shannon and Tony.

"You ready for this?" Coach asks.

Joey nods.

"You two have to work together."

Joey reaches for his toes. "I got no problem with that," he says.

"Bones?"

I look toward the East Pocono guys. "No problem," I say.

Coach is quiet for a few seconds. "Okay," he finally says.

Me and Joey walk away in opposite directions.

❀   ❀   ❀

They come out running like they did last time, keeping the ball in our end and making sharp, accurate passes. They get off a couple of good shots, but Herbie's on the spot both times. We settle down by the end of the first quarter.

Midway through the second, one of their forwards slips past Dusty with the ball and comes up the sideline into my area. He's tall and thin, with a skinny neck and a severe haircut that makes him look like a pencil. But he's quick as a whip and he gets a half step past me, and most of their team is ahead of us.

I pivot and get my foot on the ball, making him lose control. I beat him to it, and the whole field opens up in front of me. Immediately I'm in a full sprint, with Pencil Head on my tail. I hear the rising cheers as I cross midfield and angle in toward the goal. The guy is whacking me with his elbow, but I've got the ball shielded with my body.

A defender comes up to help out on me, but I see blue in the periphery of my vision. I know who it is; it has to be Joey, he's the only one who could keep up with me.

"Right here," he yells, and I pass hard with the inside of my left foot, sending the ball across the grass, five feet in front of Joey and right at the top of the goal box.

The goalie has no chance. The ball rockets past him and Joey circles around, arms in the air. Trunk races up behind him and gets him in a bear hug.

I let out my breath and shout, "Yes!"

They make some runs in the second half, but our defense is

solid. They get three or four shots on goal, but nothing too serious. Herbie is all over them.

Time is running down, but our lead doesn't feel safe. And a tie is meaningless. We have to win this one and the next or it's over.

And then it happens. Trunk takes an awkward shot and the East Pocono goalie catches it easily. He gets off a big-time punt; the ball goes way past midfield on the fly. One of their forwards gets it, but he's overanxious and boots it hard toward our goal. They've got nobody up there, so Hernandez fields it by the eighteen-yard line and makes a soft pass back to Herbie. Too soft. Pencil Head is at a full sprint, and he's going to get to the ball first. Herbie takes two steps out, sees the situation, and backs up toward the goal with his arms spread wide, crouching low.

The guy reaches the ball and gives a head fake, then fires it hard, lining it at waist level toward the goal.

Herbie gets a fist on it and it pops high into the air. It comes down and starts squibbling toward the goal, but Herbie lunges with his foot and knocks it over to the side.

Pencil Head gets there first, but Hernandez and Joey swarm all over him. He squeezes a pass to the front of the goal, and their striker receives it and shoots. Herbie's back on his feet and he dives toward the ball. He catches it and wraps his arms around it, jerking his head forward and hollering "Yeah!"

We go wild. Herbie boots it downfield. Pencil Head is shaking his head like he can't believe it. I stay back this time. They won't get in here again.

When it ends we race toward each other in an eleven-man

embrace. People pour out of the bleachers. Little brothers and sisters in skeleton masks and Muppet costumes jump into their brothers' arms.

I find Herbie and slap him on the back. "Terrific job," I say.

He shakes his head. "Unreal."

One more. The biggest one we've ever played.

I can't believe how great I feel. One good day can make a hell of a difference.

An Insider's Guide

There are three places in Sturbridge
where you can get hot-and-sour soup. One
night last summer I picked up a pint at
the China Buffet out on Route 6, Joey
bought some to go at the Ming Garden, and
we met at the little takeout place on
Main to do a taste test. I admit I went
into this with a bias toward the China
Buffet, partly because there are three
beautiful waitresses (they're sisters or
cousins) from there who go to our school.
They seem sweet, but they only recently
arrived in this country and strike me as
unapproachable.

Joey insisted that the Ming Garden's
soup would prove to be best, because
that's a classier, take-your-time kind
of restaurant. His father always brought
him there to celebrate when Joey won a
Little League championship or made a
game-winning basket or whatever. (I'm
not certain, but I think he got bread
and water at home when they lost.)

Anyway, this may not come as a huge
surprise considering the buildup, but the
simple little takeout place's soup won,
hands down—lots of flavor without scorching
your mouth. Joey described the China

Buffet's offering as "loose, brown snot in warm water." I rated the Ming Garden's stuff about a six on a scale of ten, a bit too salty and far more hot than sour. The takeout place, which has neither attractive waitresses nor comfortable ambience, certainly has the best soup.

24
THE CHAMPIONS

It's been an incredible night. Seven qualifiers in the past half hour. The count is ninety-nine. We're on our feet, gazing up and down Main Street, checking out every car. Suddenly I grab Herbie's arm and point uptown. It's Kenny, about two blocks away, leaving work and coming in this direction.

And then I look downtown and here comes Joey, walking alone, looking cocky and satisfied. I glance back at Kenny, then at Joey. They're the same distance away, in opposite directions, bearing down on us. It's like they're racing for the title.

But Kenny veers off just before he reaches us, turning in to the Turkey Hill lot. He must be getting cigarettes. And Joey is upon us, ready to be declared the victor. He stops short of me.

I look him in the eye. It's Tuesday. "Didn't you work tonight?" I ask.

"Don't work there no more."

"Why not?"

"Got fired." He looks like he's proud of it. "I told Carlos what happened."

"And?"

"I gave him fifty bucks. He said he'd forget the whole thing."

"Man, you suck. I already gave him forty."

We both laugh. Herbie pushes my head so I can see Kenny passing on the sidewalk, headed for O'Hara's Tavern. "The winner?" Herbie says.

I don't answer. I turn back to Joey. "Think we'll ever get another job in this town?" I ask.

He shrugs. "Maybe. Maybe not."

But I figure that probably isn't the worst that could happen. I mean, we're finished with that place at age fifteen. Kenny's got a lifetime sentence.

Herbie's staring at us. I grab Joey's arm and pull him aside and we start walking up Main. Herbie doesn't follow.

"Why'd you confess?" I ask.

"Got awful lonely working there."

"It's only been a couple days."

"I couldn't stand it, though," he says. "Place almost cost me a friendship."

I nod. "That and other things."

He makes one of those short, exhaley laughs, shaking his head. "Girls," he says.

"You're not giving them up, are you?" I ask.

"Not hardly," he says. He stops walking and gently swings a fist at me, hitting me in the shoulder. I swing back, bringing my fist against his.

We break into big grins. "You suck," I say, and we both know that means something else, like *We've been a couple of jerks, but let's put it behind us*. I've gained a lot in the past few months: new friends like Herbie and Rico, a tiny start toward understanding women, new confidence as an athlete. But I almost lost something that outweighs all of that, and I can tell Joey feels the same.

We walk back toward the bench.

"So who's the winner?" Herbie asks again. I stick my hand out to him. He shakes it, but he's got a puzzled look.

"I'm willing to share the title if you are," I say.

Joey puts his hand over ours and squeezes. "I'll take a piece of that, too," he says.

Herbie just shakes his head and an embarrassed smile spreads across his face. "Okay," he says. "We earned it."

25
TWENTY SECONDS

We are extremely quiet on the bus ride over to Greenfield. I'm not sure if that's good or bad. I know I'm ready to face this, even though I'm worried shit about what might happen.

We've won three straight, all by shutout, to crawl back into the race. It's down to us and them. They're a half-game ahead of us at 9–3–1; we're 8–3–2. If we lose or tie, then Greenfield takes the title. If we can pull out a win, then it's ours.

I'm sitting alone, halfway back in the bus, with my arms folded across my chest. I was really confident last night and all during the day today. I started getting nervous when I reached the locker room to change. Now I'm feeling like I could throw up any minute.

The bus pulls into the Greenfield lot and comes to a stop. Nobody moves. The sun is shining and there's not much wind and the temperature is in the upper fifties. You couldn't ask for better conditions.

Coach stands up in the aisle and rests his hands on the backs of two seats. "All right, boys," he says. "This is it."

He walks off the bus, but nobody follows right away. I glance out the window. The field is just above the Lackawanna River, and the Greenfield guys are already out there warming up. You can see the skyline of Scranton across the river, pinkish brick and gray.

I stand up, partly because we have to get out there and partly because I have to use the bathroom. I walk toward the front of the bus and the other guys follow me off.

I leave the locker room and jog the length of the field, up to our goal. The field is in perfect shape, no bare spots, just thick lush grass. It smells fresh-cut. And the bleachers are filling quickly—soccer is king over here.

Our guys are just kicking balls around and stretching, getting loose. A busload of kids from our school has arrived, and my parents and others are here, too. A jet flies low overhead toward the airport, and I hear a siren in the distance.

Joey calls my name and sends a gentle pass in the air toward me. I trap it with the inside of my foot and pass it back, then run downfield easy. Joey runs parallel to me and we pass it back and forth until we reach the opposite goal line. I circle the corner flag and head back to our end, taking a sideways glance at the Greenfield goalie, fielding shot after shot from his teammates.

The officials have arrived in their black shorts and tops, and game time is quickly approaching. I take a deep breath and stop running. Joey keeps going, dribbling toward the goal.

I bend and reach for my toes, feeling the resistance in my hamstrings when I'm about an inch above the shoes. I hold that position a few seconds, then straighten up and start bobbing side to side, building some heat.

We can beat these guys. I know we can. Even on their home field, with everything on the line, I know we can beat them.

My eyes are wide; I can feel my heart pumping. Coach calls us over and I walk toward the sideline. I am confident and ready and scared.

First quarter. Lots of nerves. We spend most of the quarter in our end, but Greenfield doesn't get off many shots. Our defenders are playing great, clearing the ball consistently, but we haven't been able to put together a string of passes yet.

Finally Rico intercepts the ball near our goal box, and their forwards quickly converge on him. He chips it to me. I settle it and turn and there's room in front of me. I'm near midfield before a Greenfield guy closes in, and I've got plenty of time to send a grass-cutting pass over to Joey. Joey one-touches it right down the field, twenty yards ahead of me and headed out of bounds. I'm in a race with one of their midfielders, but I get there first, and I cut away from the touchline, sprinting toward the goal.

I center it to Joey. Rico has run up behind me, and Joey fires it over to him. Rico receives it on the run and lines it ahead to me, and I knock it forward, chase it down, and boot it hard toward the goal.

The goalie dives toward the post, but the ball gets there first, glancing off his fingertips and rippling the back of the net. *Yes!*

Rico runs in place with his fists in the air, and I race over and bump my chest against his. And Joey's there, an arm across my back, shouting "Yeah!" as we run back upfield. We can do this.

Second quarter. Better soccer on both sides. We've got

confidence now, the nerves are gone. The Greenfield guys seem less cocky, less certain that they'll win this thing.

A Greenfield player has the ball in the far corner, trying to get away from Hernandez. He taps it up and Hernandez blocks it with his shins, but the guy regains control and for an instant has a clear look at our goal.

He lofts a soft pass right in front of the goal, about four yards in front of Herbie. Herbie freezes for a fraction of a second, not sure if he should hold his ground or make a run at the ball. Too late he darts toward it, and the Greenfield striker beats him to it. He lines a shot that Herbie takes hard in the shoulder, rolling to the ground and scrambling to his feet. But the ball spins in the air and comes down to Herbie's left, and a Greenfield player is there, the open net in front of him, and suddenly we're all tied up.

Halftime. I eat an orange and drink a pint of Gatorade. "Keep the pressure on," we're saying. Their goal was cheap, ours was solid.

"Great stop on that one before they scored," I say to Herbie.

He shrugs. "Didn't matter, though. They still put it in."

"Wasn't your fault," I say.

"It's always the goalie's fault," he says, but he doesn't seem down about it. "Just get one more. They won't put another one past me."

Third quarter. Herbie keeps his word. They get two good shots off quickly, one a header from inside the box that Herbie leaps for and catches, and the second a long, hard, low one that he stops with his outstretched hand. He falls to the ground with it, dribbling it like a basketball as he gets to his knees, then cradling it in his arms like a baby.

Then it's our turn. Joey, me, and Rico charge down the field like before, passing in a triangle and keeping the ball on the move.

We cross midfield and Dusty gets in on it, too. Joey crosses the ball to him and he cuts straight down the center, bringing us into scoring range. He back-passes to Joey, who crosses it to Rico, who gives me the same pass as before.

I receive the ball ten yards out from the goal line, about midway between the corner and the goalpost. But this time there's a defender in my face, cutting down my angle to the goal. So I move toward the goal line, planning to chip it up in front, but the guy's marking me close and I can't find a path.

I take a chance and kick it toward his skinny legs, hoping he'll deflect it back. It strikes his shin and rolls toward the goal line. He turns and chases it, and me and him and the ball reach the line at the same time. I get a foot on it and it trickles out of bounds.

The ref blows his whistle and yells, "Corner kick!"

I let out my breath. I look up at the ref and say, "Off me."

He raises his eyebrows, questioning me.

"I knocked it out," I say.

"Thank you," he says. He blows his whistle again. "Goal kick!" he yells.

My teammates groan and we trot upfield.

"Bogus call," Dusty says.

But Joey shows me his fist and nods with approval.

✪ ✪ ✪

Fourth quarter. A couple of minutes remaining. The Greenfield fans are clapping in rhythm now. All they really have to do is play defense. All they need is a tie.

They're volleying back and forth, playing keep-away instead of trying to score. We've been running our asses off, making charge after charge. They keep knocking it out of bounds or clearing it with booming kicks.

They're keeping everybody back, not even chasing those clearing kicks. Hernandez runs the ball down and dribbles till he's met at midfield by two of their forwards. He pivots and sends it over to me, and I take it into their territory but am trapped by two others.

One guy gets his foot on it and sends it back twenty yards. I run toward it, but Rico gets there first. He passes long to Trunk, who gets control and finds Joey just ahead. I'm sprinting along the sideline.

"Joey!" I yell. He gives me a lead pass and I get there first, but two green shirts converge on me and I lose it out of bounds.

They try a long throw-in. Dusty gets to it and kicks it downfield.

Time is racing away. "A tie doesn't do it!" I holler. "We gotta score!"

We're under a minute now. Our defenders come all the way down; we have to put it in the goal. Trunk passes back to Dusty, to me, to Joey. Then Dusty's in the clear, taking a long hard shot. Their goalie lunges and deflects the ball off the goalpost. And Joey is there, controlling the ball, desperate for an opening. He fires from closest range, and again it's knocked down; the goalie boots it out toward me. I stop it with my chest—it hits me hard—and I stumble back but recover. I get my foot on the ball, not quite solid, but it's on goal, high and toward the upper edge.

The goalie leaps, punches the ball over the crossbar, and I curse and swing and race toward the corner.

The referee yells, "Twenty seconds," so this is our last opportunity. I'm taking the corner kick, counting down the seconds in my head. By the time I've got the ball set there can't be more than ten seconds to go, so I'm planning to put a wicked spin on the ball, to try to hook it over the wall of defenders and into the goal.

And then I see him coming, sprinting down the field like that Mexican goalie. Herbie at full speed. So I float the ball out into the penalty area and he connects with his forehead, with all his momentum behind him, and suddenly the ball is in the net.

The ball is in the goal!

I stay in the corner. I can't move. I can't talk. They are mobbing Herbie, taking him down, jumping on each other and screaming. The ref blows his whistle; this game is history.

I sink to my knees. I lower my head and put my hands over my eyes, and I breathe deep and exhale and start sobbing.

Thank God for Mexico.

Thank God for ESPN.

I have never been so happy in my life.

GSSL Soccer Title Belongs to Sturbridge

GREENFIELD — Greenfield's five-year reign as Greater Scranton Scholastic League soccer champions came to a stunning end yesterday, as a last-second goal lifted Sturbridge to a 2–1 victory in the final regular-season game.

The winning goal came under the rarest of circumstances, with Sturbridge goalie Warren Herbert racing downfield to score off a corner kick by Barry Austin.

The victory upped the Lions' conference record to 9–3–2, a half-game better than Greenfield's mark of 9–4–1. The win also secured a spot in the district playoffs, the first ever for Sturbridge, which finished last in the conference a year ago.

"This is unreal," said Sturbridge coach Len Corupa. "When we started this program four years ago we wondered if it might take a decade or more to catch up to the established teams. But these kids decided they didn't want to wait any longer."

Corupa said that he did not instruct Herbert to leave his goal untended, but lauded his goalkeeper's action. "Herbie's always been a quick thinker. I was so intent on watching the corner kick that I didn't even see him coming. I don't know if anybody saw him."

Austin did, obviously, placing the ball perfectly for Herbert's last-second heroics.

"The ball was there; all I had to do was hit it," said

Herbert, who added that the 100-yard dash down the field was "probably the hardest I ever sprinted in my life. I figured it was now or never."

Greenfield had needed only a tie to wrap up the league title. The Mountaineers are hopeful that they'll receive an at-large bid to the playoffs.

"We just have to sit and wait," said Greenfield coach Artie Nolan. "You have to hand it to Sturbridge. They came out of nowhere this year and they gutted it out. They deserve it."

Austin had scored Sturbridge's first goal in the opening quarter, and Greenfield's Derek Masada tied the game just before the half. Greenfield appeared to have the tie in hand until a late flurry by Sturbridge. Greenfield goalie Vinnie Orr made three spectacular saves in the final seconds before Herbert's header.

"We never quit," said Herbert, who kept the Sturbridge bus waiting about ten minutes to depart as he dealt with what he dubbed "the media circus" (two daily newspapers and two weeklies covered the game; Herbert admitted that he'd never been interviewed before).

"We took a pounding last year, but we always knew we'd be OK," he said. "We started winning some this season and just kept taking it up a notch, getting more intense. We walked in here today knowing that if there was any way to win this thing, we would find it."

26
BIGGER STEPS

Monday night. Same guys on the bench: Herbie, Rico, me.

Joey and Hernandez will be along in a while.

We play at Hazleton on Thursday in the first round of the districts. Are we the same guys we were before the Greenfield game? Yes and no. I suppose we'll never really be the same.

I am proud but humbled. This was a great big step for us, but there are bigger ones ahead. I've got a lot of years of soccer still to play.

Footstepper lopes by on the other side of the street, moving quickly and silent. Going I don't know where.

Tommy drives past and hits the horn once. I put up my fist in a wave. There's a touch of winter in the air; our autumns don't last very long.

I stand and look down Main Street. There's a group of girls about a block away, mostly juniors, probably out of my league. Staci is there, the one who showed up at the Octoberfest and busted my chops about Eileen. Her friend Dana, too. I think about them sometimes.

Maybe I'll wander over there. They're laughing, having a good time. Maybe I'll walk over and say hello.

I haven't learned a damn thing, I suppose. But I guess I'm ready. Ready for something.

Ready for whatever might come next.

Special acknowledgment to Peter Dykstra, who came up with the idea of a one-hundred-person census, and actually carried the task to its stated conclusion. Unlike in this book, where the tallying takes several weeks, the town we grew up in provided all one hundred candidates during a single evening in the mid-1970s.

RICH WALLACE, the author of *Wrestling Sturbridge*, grew up in a small New Jersey town where sports were a way of life. He began writing in high school, keeping journals on the highs and lows of his life. Since then he's worked as a sportswriter, a news editor, and currently as the coordinating editor of *Highlights* magazine. As the father of two sons, he coaches a variety of youth sports, including soccer. Mr. Wallace lives in Honesdale, Pennsylvania.

WRESTLING STURBRIDGE

by Rich Wallace

Here's the deal. I'm stuck in Sturbridge, Pennsylvania, where civic pride revolves around the high school wrestling team, and the future is as bright as the inside of the cinder block factory where our dads work. And where their dads worked. And where I won't ever work. Not if I can help it.

I'm the second-best 135-pound wrestler in school, behind Al—the first-best 135-pound wrestler in the state. But I want to be state champion as badly as he does, maybe even more. I just haven't figured out how to do it.

I tell myself that I will find the way. I think my whole life depends on it.

★ "An excellent, understated first novel…Like Ben, whose voice is so strong and clear here, Wallace weighs his words carefully, making every one count." —*Booklist* (starred review)

★ "A real winner." —*Publishers Weekly* (starred review)

"There are only a few contemporary writers who can hit the mark with teenage boys, and Rich Wallace seems likely to join that group." —*Chicago Tribune*

"The author tells a terrific story—subtle, funny, cleanly drawn."
—*Los Angeles Times Book Review*

An ALA Top Ten Best Book for Young Adults
An ALA Quick Pick for Young Adults